T H E
APPOINTMENT

Born in Romania in 1953, HERTA MÜLLER lost her job as a teacher and suffered repeated threats after refusing to cooperate with Ceauşescu's Secret Police. She succeeded in emigrating in 1987 and now lives in Berlin. The recipient of the Nobel Prize in Literature and the European Literature Prize, she also won the International IMPAC Dublin Literary Award for her novel, *The Land of Green Plums* (published by Granta).

Copyright © Annette Pohnert / Carl Hanser Verlag

ALSO BY HERTA MÜLLER

The Land of Green Plums

THE
APPOINTMENT

Herta Müller

Translated from the German by Michael Hulse and Philip Boehm

Portobello
BOOKS

Published by Portobello Books Ltd 2010

Portobello Books Ltd
12 Addison Avenue
London
W11 4QR

First published in 2001 in the United States by Metropolitan Books,
Henry Holt and Company, LLC

Originally published in Germany in 1997 under the title *Heute wär ich mir
lieber nicht begegnet* by Rowohlt Verlag, Reinbek bei Hamburg

A CIP catalogue record is available from the British Library

9 8 7 6 5 4 3 2 1

ISBN 978 1 84627 276 9

www.portobellobooks.com

Offset by Avon DataSet Ltd, Bidford on Avon, Warwickshire

Printed in the UK by CPI William Clowes Beccles NR34 7TL

THE
APPOINTMENT

I've been summoned. Thursday, at ten sharp.

Lately I'm being summoned more and more often: ten sharp on Tuesday, ten sharp on Saturday, on Wednesday, Monday. As if years were a week, I'm amazed that winter comes so close on the heels of late summer.

On my way to the tram stop, I again pass the shrubs with the white berries dangling through the fences. Like buttons made of mother-of-pearl and sewn from underneath, or stitched right down into the earth, or else like bread pellets. They remind me of a flock of little white-tufted birds turning away their beaks, but they're really far too small for birds. It's enough to make you giddy. I'd rather think of snow sprinkled on the grass, but that leaves you feeling lost, and the thought of chalk makes you sleepy.

The tram doesn't run on a fixed schedule.

I

It does seem to rustle, at least to my ear, unless those are the stiff leaves of the poplars I'm hearing. Here it is, already pulling up to the stop: today it seems in a hurry to take me away. I've decided to let the old man in the straw hat get on ahead of me. He was already waiting when I arrived—who knows how long he'd been there. You couldn't exactly call him frail, but he's hunchbacked and weary, and as skinny as his own shadow. His backside is so slight it doesn't even fill the seat of his pants, he has no hips, and the only bulges in his trousers are the bags around his knees. But if he's going to go and spit, right now, just as the door is folding open, I'll get on before he does, regardless. The car is practically empty; he gives the vacant seats a quick scan and decides to stand. It's amazing how old people like him don't get tired, that they don't save their standing for places where they can't sit. Now and then you hear old people say: There'll be plenty of time for lying down once I'm in my coffin. But death is the last thing on their minds, and they're quite right. Death never has followed any particular pattern. Young people die too. I always sit if I have a choice. Riding in a seat is like walking while you're sitting down. The old man is looking me over; I can sense it right away inside the empty car. I'm not in the mood to talk, though, or else I'd ask him what he's gaping at. He couldn't care less that his staring annoys me. Meanwhile half the city is going by outside the window, trees alternating with buildings. They say old people like him can sense things better than young people. Old people might even sense that today I'm carrying a small towel, a toothbrush, and some toothpaste in my handbag. And no handkerchief, since I'm determined not to cry. Paul didn't realize how terrified I was that today Albu might take me down to the cell below his office. I didn't bring it up. If that happens, he'll find out soon enough. The tram is moving slowly. The band on the

2

old man's straw hat is stained, probably with sweat, or else the rain. As always, Albu will slobber a kiss on my hand by way of greeting.

Major Albu lifts my hand by the fingertips, squeezing my nails so hard I could scream. He presses one wet lip to my fingers, so he can keep the other free to speak. He always kisses my hand the exact same way, but what he says is always different:

Well well, your eyes look awfully red today.

I think you've got a mustache coming. A little young for that, aren't you.

My, but your little hand is cold as ice today—hope there's nothing wrong with your circulation.

Uh-oh, your gums are receding. You're beginning to look like your own grandmother.

My grandmother didn't live to grow old, I say. She never had time to lose her teeth. Albu knows all about my grandmother's teeth, which is why he's bringing them up.

As a woman, I know how I look on any given day. I also know that a kiss on the hand shouldn't hurt, that it shouldn't feel wet, that it should be delivered to the back of the hand. The art of hand kissing is something men know even better than women—and Albu is hardly an exception. His entire head reeks of Avril, a French eau de toilette that my father-in-law, the Perfumed Commissar, used to wear too. Nobody else I know would buy it. A bottle on the black market costs more than a suit in a store. Maybe it's called Septembre, I'm not sure, but there's no mistaking that acrid, smoky smell of burning leaves.

Once I'm sitting at the small table, Albu notices me rubbing my fingers on my skirt, not only to get the feeling back

3

into them but also to wipe the saliva off. He fiddles with his signet ring and smirks. Let him: it's easy enough to wipe off somebody's spit; it isn't poisonous, and it dries up all by itself. It's something everybody has. Some people spit on the pavement, then rub it in with their shoe since it's not polite to spit, not even on the pavement. Certainly Albu isn't one to spit on the pavement—not in town, anyway, where no one knows who he is and where he acts the refined gentleman. My nails hurt, but he's never squeezed them so hard my fingers turned blue. Eventually they'll thaw out, the way they do when it's freezing cold and you come into the warm. The worst thing is this feeling that my brain is slipping down into my face. It's humiliating, there's no other word for it, when your whole body feels like it's barefoot. But what if there aren't any words at all, what if even the best word isn't enough.

I've been listening to the alarm clock since three in the morning ticking ten sharp, ten sharp, ten sharp. Whenever Paul is asleep, he kicks his leg from one side of the bed to the other and then recoils so fast he startles himself, although he doesn't wake up. It's become a habit with him. No more sleep for me. I lie there awake, and I know I need to close my eyes if I'm going back to sleep, but I don't close them. I've frequently forgotten how to sleep, and have had to relearn each time. It's either extremely easy or utterly impossible. In the early hours just before dawn, every creature on earth is asleep: even dogs and cats only use half the night for prowling around the dumpsters. If you're sure you can't sleep anyway, it's easier to think of something bright inside the darkness than to simply shut your eyes in vain. Snow, whitewashed tree trunks, white-walled rooms, vast expanses of sand—that's what I've thought of to

4

pass the time, more often than I would have liked, until it grew light. This morning I could have thought about sunflowers, and I did, but they weren't enough to dislodge the summons. And with the alarm clock ticking ten sharp, ten sharp, ten sharp, my thoughts raced to Major Albu even before they shifted to me and Paul. Today I was already awake when Paul started thrashing in his sleep. By the time the window started turning gray, I had already seen Albu's mouth looming on the ceiling, gigantic, the pink tip of his tongue tucked behind his lower teeth, and I had heard his sneering voice:

Don't tell me you're losing your nerve already—we're just warming up.

Paul's kicking wakes me only when I haven't been summoned for two or three weeks. Then I feel happy, since it means I've learned how to sleep again.

Whenever I've relearned how to sleep, and I ask Paul in the morning what he was dreaming, he can't remember anything. I show him how he tosses about and splays his toes, and then how he jerks his legs back and crooks his toes. Moving a chair from the table to the middle of the kitchen, I sit down, stick my legs in the air, and demonstrate the whole procedure. It makes Paul laugh, and I say:

You're laughing at yourself.

Who knows, maybe I dreamed I was taking you for a ride on my motorcycle.

His thrashing is like a forward charge disrupted by an immediate call to retreat. I presume it comes from drinking. Not that I say this to him. Nor do I explain that it's the night drawing the shakes out of his legs. That's what it must be—the night, seizing him by the knees and tugging at the shakes, pulling them down through his toes into the pitch-black room, and finally tossing them out into the blackness of the street below, in the early hours just before daybreak, when the whole city is slumbering away. Otherwise Paul wouldn't be able to stand up straight when he woke. But if night wrenches the shakes out of every drunk in the city, it must be tanked up to high heaven come morning, given the number of drinkers.

Just after four, the trucks begin delivering goods to the row of shops down below. They completely shatter the silence, making a huge racket for the little they deliver: a few crates of bread, milk, and vegetables, and large quantities of plum brandy. Whenever the food runs out, the women and children manage to cope: the lines disperse, and all roads lead home. But when the brandy runs out, the men curse their lot and pull out their knives. The salespeople say things to calm them down, but that only works while the customers are still inside the store. The moment they're out the door they continue prowling the city on their quest. The first fights break out because they can't find any brandy, and later because they're stone drunk.

The brandy comes from the hilly region between the Carpathians and the arid plains. The plum trees there are so dense you can barely make out the tiny villages hiding in their branches. Whole forests of plum trees, drenched with blue in late summer, the branches sagging with the weight of the fruit. The brandy is named after the region, but nobody calls it by its proper name. It doesn't really even need a name, since there's only one brand in the whole country. People just call it Two Plums, from the picture on the label. Those two plums leaning cheek to cheek are as familiar to the men as the Madonna and Child are to the women. People say the plums represent the love between bottle and drinker. The way I see it, those cheek-to-cheek plums look more like a wedding picture than a Madonna and Child. None of the pictures in church shows the Child's head level with his mother's. The Child's forehead is

6

always resting against the Virgin's cheek, with his own cheek at her neck, and his chin on her breast. Moreover, the relationship between drinkers and bottles is more like the one between the couples in wedding pictures: they bring each other to ruin, and still they won't let go.

In our wedding picture, I'm not carrying flowers and I'm not wearing a veil. The love in my eyes is gleaming new, but the truth is, it was my second wedding. The picture shows Paul and me standing cheek to cheek like two plums. Ever since he started drinking so much, our wedding picture has proven prophetic. Whenever Paul's out on the town, barhopping late into the night, I'm afraid he'll never come home again, and I stare at our wedding picture until it starts to change shape. When that happens our two faces start to swim, and our cheeks shift around so that a little bit of space opens up between them. Mostly it is Paul's cheek that swims away from mine, as if he were planning to come home late. But he does come home. He always has, even after the accident.

Occasionally a shipment of buffalo-grass vodka comes in from Poland—yellowish and bittersweet. That gets sold first. Each bottle contains a long, sodden stem that quivers as you pour the vodka but never buckles or slips out of the bottle. Drinkers say:

That stem sticks in its bottle just like your soul sticks in your body, that's how the grass protects your soul.

Their belief goes together with the burning taste in your mouth and the roaring drunk inside your head. The drinkers open the bottle, the liquid glugs into their glasses, and the first swallow slides down their throats. The soul begins to feel protected; it quivers but never buckles and never slips out of the body. Paul keeps his soul protected too; there's never a day where he feels like giving up and packing it all in. Maybe things would be fine if it weren't for me, but we like being together. The drink takes his day, and the night takes his drunkenness. When I worked the early morning shift at the clothing factory, I heard the workers say: With a sewing machine, you oil the cogs, with a human machine, you oil the throat.

Back then Paul and I used to take his motorcycle to work every morning at five on the dot. We'd see the drivers with their delivery trucks parked outside the stores, the porters carrying crates, the vendors, and the moon. Now all I hear is the noise; I don't go to the window, and I don't look at the moon. I remember that it looks like a goose egg, and that it leaves the city on one side of the sky while the sun comes up at the other. Nothing's changed there; that's how it was even before I knew Paul, when I used to walk to the tram stop on foot. On the way I thought: How bizarre that something so beautiful could be up in the sky, with no law down here on earth forbidding people to look at it. Evidently it was permissible to wangle something out of the day before it was ruined in the factory. I would start to freeze, not because I was underdressed, but simply because I couldn't get enough of the moon. At that hour the moon is almost entirely eaten away; it doesn't know where to go after reaching the city. The sky has to loosen its grip on the earth as day begins to break. The streets run steeply up and down, and the streetcars travel back and forth like rooms ablaze with light.

I know the trams from the inside too. The people getting on at this early hour wear short sleeves, carry worn leather bags, and have goose pimples on both arms. Each newcomer is measured and judged with a casual glance. This is a strictly working-class affair. Better people take their cars to work. But here, among your own, you make comparisons: that person's better off than me, that one looks worse. No one's ever in the exact same boat as you—that would be impossible. There's not much time, we're almost at the factories, and now all the people who've been sized up leave the tram, one after the other. Shoes polished or dusty, heels new and straight or worn down to an angle, collars freshly ironed or crumpled, hair parted or not, fingernails, watchstraps, belt buckles: every single detail provokes envy or contempt. Nothing escapes this sleepy scrutiny, even in the pushing crowd. The working class ferrets out the differences: in the cold light of morning there is no equality. The sun is in the streetcar, along for the ride, and outside as well, pulling back the white and red clouds in anticipation of the scorching midday heat. No one is wearing a jacket: the freezing cold in the morning counts as fresh air, because with noon will come the clogging dust and infernal heat.

If I haven't been summoned, we can sleep in for several hours. Daytime sleep is not deep black; it's shallow and yellow. Our sleep is restless, the sunlight falls on our pillows. But it does make the day a little shorter. We'll be under observation soon enough; the day's not going to run away. They can always accuse us of something, even if we sleep till nearly noon. As it is, we're always being accused of something we can no longer do anything about. You can sleep all you want, but the day's still out there waiting, and a bed is not another country. They won't let us rest till we're lying next to Lilli.

Of course Paul also has to sleep off his drunk. It takes him until about noon to get his head square on his shoulders and relocate his mouth so he can actually speak and not just slur his words in a voice thick with drink. His breath still smells, though, and when he steps into the kitchen I feel as if I were passing the open door of the bar downstairs. Since spring, drinking hours have been regulated, and consumption of liquor is prohibited before eleven. But the bar still opens at six—brandy is served in coffee cups before eleven; after that they bring out the glasses.

Paul drinks and is no longer himself, then he sleeps it off and is back to being himself. Around noon it looks as if everything could turn out all right, but once again it turns out ruined. Paul goes on protecting his soul until the buffalo grass is high and dry, while I brood over who he and I really are until I can no longer think straight. At lunchtime we're sitting at the kitchen table, and any mention of his having been drunk yesterday is the wrong thing to say. Even so, I occasionally toss out a word or two:

Drink won't change a thing.

Why are you making my life so difficult.

You could paint this entire kitchen with what you put away yesterday.

True, the flat is small, and I don't want to avoid Paul; but when we stay at home, we spend too much of the day sitting in the kitchen. By mid-afternoon he's already drunk, and in the evening it gets worse. I put off talking because it makes him grumpy. I keep waiting through the night, until he's sober again and sitting in the kitchen with eyes like onions. But then whatever I say goes right past him. I'd like for Paul to admit I'm right, just for once. But drinkers never admit anything, not even silently to themselves—and they're not about to let anyone else squeeze it out of them, especially somebody who's waiting to hear the admission. The minute Paul wakes up, his thoughts turn to drinking, though he denies it. That's why there's never any truth. If he's not sitting silently at the table, letting my words go right past him, he says something like this, meant to last the entire day:

Don't fret, I'm not drinking out of desperation. I drink because I like it.

That may be the case, I say, since you seem to think with your tongue.

Paul looks out the kitchen window at the sky, or into his cup. He dabs at the drops of coffee on the table, as if to confirm that they're wet and really will spread if he smears them with a finger. He takes my hand, I look out the kitchen window at the sky, into the cup, I too dab at the odd drop of coffee on the table. The red enamel tin stares at us and I stare back. But Paul does not, because that would mean doing something different today from what he did yesterday. Is he being strong or weak when he remains silent instead of saying for once: I'm not going to drink today. Yesterday Paul again said:

Don't you fret, your man drinks because he likes it.

His legs carried him down the hall—at once too heavy and too light—as if they contained a mix of sand and air. I placed my hand upon his neck and stroked the stubble I love to touch in the mornings, the whiskers that grow in his sleep. He drew my hand up under his eye, it slid down his cheek to his chin. I didn't take away my fingers, but I did think to myself:

I wouldn't count on any of this cheek-to-cheek business after you've seen that picture of the two plums.

I like to hear Paul talk that way, so late in the morning, and yet I don't like it either. Whenever I take a step away from him, he nudges his love up to me, so naked, so close that he doesn't need to say anything else. He doesn't have to wait, I'm ready with my approval, not a single reproach on the tip of my tongue. The one in my head quickly fades. It's good I can't see myself, since my face feels stupid and pale. Yesterday morning, Paul's hangover once again yielded up an unexpected pussycat gentleness that came padding on soft paws. *Your man*—the only people who talk like that have shallow wits and too much pride tucked around the corners of their mouths. Although the noontime tenderness paves the way for the evening's drinking, I depend on it, and I don't like the way I need it.

Major Albu says: I can see what you're thinking, there's no point in denying it, we're just wasting time. Actually, it's only my time being wasted; after all, he's doing his job. He rolls up his sleeve and glances at the clock. The time is easy to see, but not what I'm thinking. If Paul can't see what I'm thinking, then certainly this man can't.

Paul sleeps next to the wall, while my place is toward the front edge of the bed, since I'm often unable to sleep. Still, whenever he wakes up he says:

You were taking up the whole bed and shoved me right up against the wall.

To which I reply:

No way, I was on this little strip here no wider than a clothesline, you were the one taking up the middle.

One of us could sleep in the bed and the other on the sofa. We've tried it. For two nights we took turns. Both nights I did nothing but toss around. My brain was grinding down thought after thought, and toward morning, when I was half asleep, I had a series of bad dreams. Two nights of bad dreams that kept reaching out and clutching at me all day long. The night I was on the sofa, my first husband put the suitcase on the bridge over the river, gripped me by the back of my neck, and roared with laughter. Then he looked at the water and whistled that song about love falling apart and the river water turning black as ink. The water in my dream was not like ink, I could see it, and in the water I saw his face, turned upside down and peering up from the depths, from where the pebbles had settled. Then a white horse ate apricots in a thicket of trees. With every apricot it raised its head and spat out the stone like a human being. And the night I had the bed to myself, someone grabbed my shoulder from behind and said:

Don't turn around, I'm not here.

Without moving my head, I just squinted out of the corners of my eyes. Lilli's fingers were gripping me, her voice was that of a man, so it wasn't her. I raised my hand to touch her and the voice said:

What you can't see you can't touch.

I saw the fingers, they were hers, but someone else was using them. Someone I couldn't see. And in the next dream, my grandfather was pruning back a hydrangea that had been frost-burnt by the snow. He called me over: Come take a look, I've got a lamb here.

Snow was falling on his trousers, his shears were clipping off the heads of the frost-browned flowers. I said:

That's not a lamb.

It's not a person, either, he said.

His fingers were numb and he could only open and close the shears slowly, so that I wasn't sure whether it was the shears that were squeaking or his hand. I tossed the shears into the snow. They sank in so that it was impossible to tell where they had fallen. He combed the entire yard looking for them, his nose practically touching the snow. When he reached the garden gate I stepped on his hands so he'd look up and not go wandering off through the gate, searching the whole white street. I said:

Stop it, the lamb's frozen and the wool got burnt in the frost.

By the garden fence was another hydrangea, one that had been pruned bare. I gestured to it:

What's wrong with that one.

13

That one's the worst, he said. Come spring it'll be having little ones. We can't have that.

The morning after the second night, Paul said:

⌐ If we're in each other's way, at least it means we each have someone. The only place you sleep alone is in your coffin, and that'll happen soon enough. We should stay together at night. ⌐Who knows the dreams he had and promptly forgot.

He was talking about sleeping, however, not dreaming. At half past four in the morning I saw Paul asleep in the gray light, a twisted face above a double chin. And at that early hour, down by the shops, people were cursing out loud and laughing. Lilli said:

Curses ward off evil spirits.

Idiot, get your foot out of the way. Move, or do you have shit in your shoes. Open those great flapping ears of yours and you'll hear what I'm saying, but watch you don't blow away in this wind. Never mind your hair, we haven't finished unloading. A woman was clucking, short and hoarse like a hen. A van door slammed. Lend a hand, you moron. If you want a rest you should check into a sanatorium.

Paul's clothes were strewn on the floor. The new day was already in the wardrobe mirror, the day on which I have been summoned, today. I got up, careful to place my right foot on the floor before my left, as I always do when I've been summoned. I can't say for sure I really believe in it, but how could it hurt.

What I'd like to know is whether other people's brains control their good fortune as well as their thoughts. My brain's only good for a little fortune. It's not up to shaping a whole life. At least not mine. I've already come to terms with what fortune I have, even though Paul wouldn't consider it very good at all. Every other day or so I declare:

I'm doing just fine.

Paul's face is right in front of me, quiet and still, gaping at what I've just said, as if our having each other didn't count. He says:

You feel fine because you've forgotten what that means for other people.

Others might mean their life as a whole when they say: I'm doing just fine. All I'm talking about is my good fortune. Paul realizes that life is something I haven't come to terms with—and I don't simply mean I haven't done so yet, that it's only a matter of time.

Just look at us, says Paul, how can you go on about being fortunate.

Quick as a handful of flour hitting a windowpane, the bathroom light cast a face into the mirror, a face with froggy creases over its eyes which looked like me. I held my hands in the water, it felt warm; on my face it felt cold. Brushing my teeth, I look up and see toothpaste come frothing out of my eyes—it's not the first time I've had this happen. I feel nauseous, I spit out what's in my mouth and stop. Ever since my first summons, I've begun to distinguish between life and fortune. When I go in for questioning, I have no choice but to leave my good fortune at home. I leave it in Paul's face, around his eyes, his mouth, amid his stubble. If it could be seen, you'd see it on his face like a transparent glaze. Every time I have to go, I want to stay behind in the flat, like the fear I always leave behind and which I can't take away from Paul. Like the fortune I leave at home when I'm away. He doesn't know how much my good fortune has come to rely upon his fear. He couldn't bear to know that. What he does know is obvious to anyone with eyes: that whenever I've been summoned, I put on my green blouse and eat a walnut. The blouse is one I inherited from Lilli, but its name comes from me: the blouse that grows. If I were to take my good fortune with me, it would weaken my nerves. Albu says:

You don't mean you're losing your nerve already—we're just warming up.

I'm not losing my nerve, not at all: in fact, I'm overloaded with nerves. And every one of them is humming like a moving streetcar.

They say that walnuts on an empty stomach are good for your nerves and your powers of reason. Any child knows that, but I'd forgotten it. What sparked my memory wasn't the fact that I was being summoned so often—it was sheer chance. One time I had to be at Albu's at ten sharp, like today; by half past seven I was all set to go. Getting there takes an hour and a half at most. I give myself two hours, and if I'm early I walk a while around the neighborhood. I prefer it that way. I've always arrived on time: I can't imagine they'd put up with any lateness.

It was because I was all set to go by half past seven that I got to eat the walnut. I'd been ready that early for previous summonses, but on that particular morning the walnut was lying there on the kitchen table. Paul had found it in the elevator the day before. He'd put it in his pocket, since you don't just leave a walnut sitting there. It was the first one of the year, with a little of the moist fuzz left from the green husk. I weighed it in my hand: it seemed a little light for a good fresh nut, as if it might be hollow. I couldn't find a hammer, so I split it open with the stone that used to be in the hall but has since moved to a corner of the kitchen. The brain of the nut was loose inside. It tasted of sour cream. That day my interrogation was shorter than usual, I kept my nerve, and once I was back on the street, I thought to myself:

That was thanks to the nut.

Ever since then I've believed in nuts, that nuts help. I don't really believe it, but I want to have done whatever I can that might help. That's why I stick to my stone for cracking nuts, and always do it in the morning. Once the nut's been cracked, it loses its power if it lies open overnight. Of course it would be easier on Paul and the neighbors—not to mention myself—if I split them open in the evening, but I can't have people telling me what time to crack nuts.

I brought the stone from the Carpathians. My first husband had been on military service since March. Every week he wrote me a whining letter and I responded with a comforting card. Summer came, and I tried to figure out exactly how many letters and cards we would have to exchange before he returned. My father-in-law wanted to take his place and sleep with me, so I soon had enough of his house and garden. I packed my rucksack and early one morning, after he'd gone to work, I stashed it in the bushes near a gap in the fence. A few hours later I strolled out to the road, with nothing in my hands. My mother-in-law was hanging out the laundry and had no idea what I was up to. Without saying a word, I pushed the rucksack through the gap in the fence and walked to the station. I took a train into the mountains and joined up with some people who'd just graduated from the music academy. Every day we trekked and stumbled from one glacial lake to the next until it grew dark. Each shoreline was marked by wooden crosses set in the rocks, bearing the dates on which people had drowned. Cemeteries underwater and crosses all around—portents of dangerous times to come. As if all those round lakes were hungry and needed their yearly ration of meat delivered on the dates inscribed. Here no one dived for the dead: the water would snuff out life in an instant, chilling you to the bone in a matter of seconds. The music graduates sang as the lake pictured them, upside down, taking their measure as potential corpses. Hiking, resting, or eating, they sang in chorus. It wouldn't have surprised me to hear them harmonize while they slept at night, just as they did at those bleak altitudes where the sky blows into your mouth. I had to stay with the group because death makes no allowance for the wanderer who strays alone. The lakes made our eyes grow bigger by the day; in every face I could see the circles widening, the cheeks losing ground. And every day our legs grew shorter. Nevertheless, on the last day I wanted to take something back home with me, so I picked through the scree until I found a rock that looked like a child's foot. The musicians looked for small flat pebbles they could rub in their hands as worry-stones. Their stones looked like coat buttons, and I had more than enough of those every day in the factory. But those musicians put their faith in worry-stones the way I now put mine in nuts.

I can't help it: I've put on the blouse that grows, I bang twice with the stone, rattling all the dishes in the kitchen, and the walnut is cracked. And as I'm eating it, Paul comes in, startled by the banging. He's wearing his pajamas and downs one or two glasses of water, two if he was as blind drunk as he was last night. I don't need to understand each individual word. I know perfectly well what he says while drinking water:

You don't really believe that nut helps, do you.

Of course I don't really believe it, just as I don't really believe in all the other routines I've developed. Consequently I'm all the more stubborn.

Let me believe what I want.

Paul lets that one go, since we both know it's not right to quarrel before the interrogation, you need to keep a clear head. Most of the sessions are torturously long despite the nut. But how do I know they wouldn't be worse if I didn't eat the nut? Paul doesn't realize that the more he pooh-poohs all my routines, with that wet mouth of his and the glass he's draining before clearing it off the table, the more I rely on them.

People who are summoned develop routines that help them out a little. Whether these routines really work or not is beside the point. It's not people, though, it's me who's developed them; they came sneaking up on me, one by one.

Paul says:

The things you waste your time on.

What he does, instead, is consider what questions they'll ask me when I'm summoned. This is absolutely necessary, he claims, whereas what I do is crazy. He'd be right if the questions he's preparing me for really were the ones I was asked. Up to now they've always been completely different.

It's too much to expect my routines to really help me. Actually they don't help me so much as help move life along from one day to the next. There's no point expecting them to fill your head with lucky thoughts. There's a lot to be said for moving life along, but there's essentially nothing to say when it comes to luck, because as soon as you open your mouth you jinx it away. Not even the luck you've missed out on can bear being talked about. The routines I've developed are about moving from one day to the next, and not about luck.

I'm sure Paul's right: the walnut and the blouse that grows only add to the fear. And what sense is there in shooting for good fortune when all that does is add to the fear. I am constantly dwelling on this, and as a result I don't expect as much as other people. Nobody covets the fear that others make for themselves. But with luck it's just the opposite, which is why good fortune is never a very good goal.

On the green blouse that grows there's a large mother-of-pearl button which I picked out from a great many buttons at the factory and took for Lilli.

At the interrogation I sit at the small table, twisting the button in my fingers, and answer calmly, even though every one of my nerves is jangling. Albu paces to and fro; having to formulate the right questions wears at his calm, just as having to give the right answers wears at mine. As long as I keep my composure there's the chance he'll get something wrong—maybe everything. Back home I change into my gray blouse. This one's called the blouse that waits. It's a gift from Paul. Of course I often have misgivings about these names. But they've never done any harm, not even on days when I haven't been summoned. The blouse that grows helps me, and the blouse that waits may be helping Paul. His fear on my behalf is as high as the ceiling, just as mine is for him when he sits around the flat, waiting and drinking, or when he's barhopping in town. It's easier if you're the one going out, if you're the one taking your fear away and leaving your fortune at home, and if there's someone waiting for you to come back. Sitting at home, waiting, stretches time to the brink and tightens fear to the point of snapping.

The powers I've bestowed on my routines verge on the superhuman. Albu yells:

You see, everything is connected.

And I twist the large button on my blouse and say: In your mind they are, in my mind they aren't.

Shortly before he got off, the old man in the straw hat turned his watery eyes away from me. Now there's a father with a child on his lap sitting on the seat facing me, his legs stretched out into the aisle. Watching the city go by outside the window isn't something he can be bothered with. The child sticks a forefinger up his father's nose. Crooking a finger and hunting for snot is something kids learn early. Later they're told not to pick anyone's nose but their own, and then only if no one's watching. This father doesn't think that later has arrived yet; he smiles, perhaps he's enjoying it. The tram halts in the middle of the tracks, between stops, the driver gets out. Who knows how long we'll be stranded. It's early in the morning and already he's sneaking a break when he should be driving his route. Everyone here does what he wants. The driver strolls over to the shops, tucking in his shirt and adjusting his trousers so no one will notice he's abandoned his tram in mid-route. He acts like someone who's so bored that he finally got up off his couch just to poke his nose into the sunshine. If he's planning to buy anything in one of the shops over there, he'll either have to say who he is or else he'll have to wait in line. If all he's after is a cup of coffee, I hope he doesn't sit down to drink it. He doesn't dare touch brandy, even if he does keep his window open. Every one of us sitting on the tram has the right to reek of brandy except for him. But he's behaving as if it were the other way round. My summons puts me in the same position as far as brandy is concerned. I'd rather have his reason for abstaining than my own. Who knows when he'll be back.

Ever since I began leaving my good fortune at home, the kiss on my hand doesn't paralyze me as much as it used to. I crook up my finger joints so that my knuckles keep Albu from speaking. Paul and I have rehearsed this kiss. In order to approximate the importance of the signet ring on Albu's middle finger, to see how it affects the finger-squeeze, I made a ring out of a strip of rubber and a coat button. We took turns wearing it, and we laughed so much we completely forgot why we were going through the exercise in the first place. I learned not to crook my hand up all at once but gradually. That way the knuckles can block his gums and keep him from speaking. Sometimes when Albu is kissing my hand, I think of my rehearsal with Paul. Then the pain at my fingernails and the slobber on my hand aren't so humiliating. You learn as you go, but I can't show that I'm learning, and whatever happens I cannot laugh.

ᒥ If you're walking or driving around the leaning tower, where Paul and I live, you can't really keep more than the entranceway and the lower stories under surveillance. From the sixth floor up the flats are too high, so that you'd need sophisticated technology to see anything in detail. What's more, about halfway up the building, the façade angles out toward the front. If you stare up at it long enough you'll feel your eyes rolling back into your forehead. I've tried it often; your neck grows tired. The leaning tower has looked like that for twelve years now, says Paul, from the day it was built. Whenever I want to explain where I live, all I have to do is say: In the leaning tower. Everyone in the city knows where it is. They ask:

Aren't you afraid it might collapse.

I'm not afraid, I say, it was built with reinforced concrete.

Whenever I refer to the tower, people look down at the floor, as if looking at me might make them dizzy, so I say:

Everything else in this city will collapse first.

At that they nod, to relax the veins that are twitching in their necks.

The fact that our flat is high up is an advantage for us, but it also has the disadvantage that Paul and I can't see exactly what's going on down below. From the seventh floor you can't make out anything smaller than a suitcase, and when do you see anyone carrying a suitcase. Individual items of clothing blur into big splotches of color, and faces turn into little pale patches between the hair and the clothes. You could guess at what the nose, eyes, or teeth inside those patches might look like, but why bother. Old people and children can be recognized by the way they walk. There are dumpsters located on the grass between our building and the shops, with a walkway running alongside them. Two narrow footpaths leave the paved sidewalk and circle around the group of bins, without quite meeting. From up here the bins look like ransacked cupboards with the doors torn off. Once a month someone sets them on fire, the smoke rises and the garbage is consumed. If your windows aren't shut, your eyes start stinging and your throat gets sore. Most things happen outside the entrances to the shops, but unfortunately all we can see are the rear service doors. No matter how often we count them, we can never match up the twenty-seven doors in back with the eight front doors belonging to the grocer, the bread shop, the greengrocer, the pharmacy, the bar, the shoemaker, the hairdresser, and the kindergarten. The whole rear wall is riddled with doors; nevertheless, the delivery trucks stop mostly in the street, out front.

The old shoemaker was complaining he had too little room and too many rats. His shop consists of a workbench enclosed in a small space that is partitioned from the rest of the room by a makeshift wall of wooden planks. The man I took over from was the one who fixed the place up, the shoemaker said. Back then the building was new. The space was boarded off then too, but he couldn't think of anything to do with all those planks, or maybe he just didn't want to; anyway, he didn't use them at all. I knocked in a few nails and ever since I've been hanging the shoes up by their laces, thongs, or heels, they don't get gnawed on anymore. I can't have the rats eating everything—

after all, I have to pay for the damage. Especially in winter, when they're hungrier. Behind those planks there's a great big hall. Once, back in the early days, during a holiday, I came down to the shop, loosened two of the boards behind the bench, and squeezed through with a flashlight. There's nowhere you can put your feet, the whole floor skitters and squeaks, he said, it's full of rats' nests. Rats don't need a door, you know, they just tunnel through the ground. The walls are covered with electrical sockets, and the back wall has four doors leading out to the bins. But you can't budge them so much as an inch to drive the rats out even for a couple hours. The door to my workplace is just a cheap piece of tin—in fact, more than half the doors in back of the shops aren't doors at all, they're just tin plates they built into the wall to save on concrete. The sockets are probably there in case of war. There'll always be war all right, he laughed, but not here. The Russians've got us where they want us with treaties, they won't be showing up here. Whatever they need, they've shipped off to Moscow: they eat our grain and our meat and leave us to go hungry and fight over the shortages. Who'd want to conquer us, all it would do is cost them money. Every country on earth is happy not to have us, even the Russians.

The driver returns, eating a crescent roll, in no particular hurry. His shirt has slipped back outside his trousers, as if he'd been driving the whole time. His cheeks are stuffed with food, he runs his hand through his hair, clutching a half-eaten roll and making more of a face than the effort of chewing calls for. Now he tidies up on the step up to the car, although not for us. For us he puts on a grouchy face so no one in the tram will dare utter a word. He climbs in, his other hand holding a second roll, while a third is poking out of his shirt pocket. Slowly the tram starts moving. The father with the boy has taken his legs out of the aisle and stretched them between the seats. His son is licking the pane, but instead of pulling the boy away, the man is holding the little one's neck so his little bright-red tongue can reach the window. The boy turns his head, stares, grabs his father's ear, and babbles. The father doesn't bother to wipe the dribble off the boy's chin. Maybe he's actually listening. But his thoughts are clearly elsewhere as he stares out through the saliva smeared on the windowpane, as if it were perfectly normal for windows to drool. The hair at the back of his head is shorn close, like on a pelt. Running through it is the bald line of a scar.

For a whole week, when summer came and people began running around in short sleeves, Paul and I were suspicious of a man who to this day walks over from the shops every morning at ten to eight, empty-handed. Every day he steps off the paved sidewalk and follows the paths around the dumpsters and then steps back on the sidewalk and returns to the shops. At one point Paul couldn't stand it any longer, he stuffed some paper in a plastic bag and set out to follow the man. He didn't come back until lunch, equipped with a long white loaf of the kind you can carry under your arm. With that he headed for the street the next morning at a quarter past seven, and at ten to eight, after the man had completed his circuit of the dumpsters, Paul returned with the same loaf of bread, now broken in two. Evidently the man is about forty, wears a cross on a gold chain, has an anchor tattooed on one inner arm and the name Ana on the other. He lives in a bright-green row house on Mulberry Street and every morning, before he makes his circuit of the dumpsters, he drops off a blubbering boy at the kindergarten. There's no reason for him to pass by our tower on his way home from the kindergarten, unless he just wants a change of pace. Though it's hardly a change if you take the same detour every single day. Paul says:

The man walks by the trash cans because they're near a bar he just passed that's nagging at him. The brandy-like smell of fermenting garbage somehow eases his guilty conscience, so he does an about-face and orders his first brandy of the day in the bar. The rest of the glasses follow automatically. Around nine o'clock he's joined by another man wearing a short-sleeved brown summer suit, who only drinks two cups of coffee but stays at the man's table until five to twelve, when it's time to pick up the child. The boy is still crying at noon, when he sees the man waiting for him.

To my nose the trash cans don't stink of brandy, but drinkers may have a different sense of smell. Still, why does the man insist on craning his neck and looking up while he's making his rounds down there. And who is that person who keeps him company in the bar. I suspect Paul has himself in mind when he says that the man is lifting his head up to heaven as he heads home, in order to stave off the guilt he feels at hitting the booze. And why does the child cry when he sees him, maybe he doesn't belong to the man at all. Paul has no idea but says:

Who'd borrow a kid.

Obviously Paul never does the shopping, or else he'd know that people really do borrow children to get larger rations of meat, milk, and bread in the shops.

Why does Paul say this drinker goes to such and such a place every morning when in fact he only followed the man for one morning and part of an afternoon. It could all be coincidence rather than habit. Albu is trained to notice such things.

At varying intervals, and just to confuse me, he asks the same thing at least three times before he's satisfied with the answer. Only then does he say:

You see, things are getting connected.

Paul says I should follow the alcoholic myself if I'm not satisfied with his report. But I'd rather not. A bag in your hand and a loaf under your arm doesn't make you invisible; it could easily give you away.

I no longer stand beside our window at ten to eight, although every morning it occurs to me that the man is walking around down there, craning his neck. Nor do I say anything anymore, because Paul digs in so, insisting he's right, as if he needs this drinker in his life more than he needs me. As if our life would be easier if the man caught between his child and his drink were simply a tormented father.

That may all be true, I say, but he still might be doing a little spying on the side.

Now the driver has scratched the salt off his second crescent roll. The coarse grains burn your tongue and ruin the enamel on your teeth. And salt makes you thirsty, maybe he doesn't want to be drinking water all the time, because he can't go to the toilet while he's on duty, and because the more you drink the more you sweat. My grandfather told me that in the camp they used salt from evaporated water to clean their teeth. They would take it in their mouth and rub it over their teeth with the tip of their tongue. But that salt was as fine as dust. After the driver finished his first roll he swigged something from a bottle. Water, I hope.

A truck full of sheep crosses the intersection. The sheep are crammed in so tight they can't fall over no matter how bumpy the ride. No heads, no bellies, just black and white wool. Only when we take the turn do I notice a dog's head in their midst. And a man in a small green climbing cap, the kind that shepherds wear, sitting in the cab, next to the driver. They're probably moving the flock to a new pasture—you don't need a dog at the slaughterhouse.

Some things aren't bad until you start talking about them. I've learned how to hold my tongue before it gets me into trouble, but usually it's already too late, because sooner or later I always want to have my say. Whenever Paul and I don't understand something that troubles other people, we start to quarrel. Things quickly escalate until they get out of hand, and every ⌈salvo calls for an even more thunderous one in return. I think we see in that alcoholic man the things that most torment us, and these things are different for each of us, despite our com-⌊mon love. Evidently drinking troubles Paul more than my being summoned. He drinks the most whenever I'm summoned, and on those days especially I have no right to reproach him for his drinking, even though his being drunk troubles me more than . . .

My first husband also had a tattoo. He returned home from the army with a rose threaded through a heart inked on his chest. My name beneath the stem. But I left him nevertheless.

Why in the world have you gone and ruined your skin. The only place that rosy heart might possibly look right is on your gravestone.

Because the days were long and I was thinking of you, he explained, and everybody else was getting one. Apart from the chickenhearts. We had our share of those, just like anywhere else.

28

I didn't leave him for some other man, as he suspected, I just wanted to leave him. He wanted an itemized list of the reasons why. I couldn't spell out a single one.

Are you disappointed in me, he asked. Or have I changed.

No, we were both exactly the same as when we met. Love can't go on just running in place, but that's what our love had been doing for two and a half years. He looked at me, and when I said nothing, he declared:

You're one of those who needs a good beating now and then, only I wasn't up to giving it to you.

He meant it, since he knew he could never raise a hand against me. I believed it too. Up to that day on the bridge he wasn't even capable of slamming a door in anger.

It was already half past seven in the evening. He asked me to dash out with him to buy a suitcase before the shops closed. He was planning to leave the next day for a two-week trip to the mountains. He expected me to miss him. But two weeks is nothing. Even our two and a half years weren't much.

We left the store and walked through the city in silence. He was carrying the new suitcase. The shop had been about to close and the salesgirl hadn't cleaned out the case, it was stuffed full of paper and had a price tag dangling from the handle. The previous day there had been a downpour, the high, silty water was tearing at the willows along the river. Halfway across the bridge he stopped and squeezed my arm. He was kneading my flesh so hard, down to the bone, that I shuddered, and he said:

Look at all that water. If I come back from the mountains and find you've left me, I'll jump right in.

The suitcase was suspended between us; behind him I could see water, and branches, and muddy scum. I yelled:

You can jump right now, with me watching. Then you won't have to bother going to the mountains.

I took a deep breath and lowered my head. It wasn't my fault if he thought I wanted a kiss. He parted his lips, but I repeated:

Go on and jump. I'll take full responsibility.

Then I jerked my arm away so both his hands were free and he could jump. I was numb with the fear that he'd actually do it. Then I walked on, taking short steps, without looking back, so he wouldn't have to feel awkward, and so I'd be far enough away from the body. I'd nearly reached the far side of the bridge when he came panting after me and shoved me up against the railing, crushing my belly. He grabbed me by the back of my neck and forced my head down toward the water as far as his arm would let him. The whole weight of my body was hanging over the railing, my feet were off the ground, he kept his knees clamped tight around my calves. I shut my eyes and waited for a final word before I plummeted. He kept it short and said:

All right.

Who can say why instead of loosening his knees to let me drop he relaxed his grip on my neck, lowered me to the ground, and took a step away. I opened my eyes and slowly they rolled back down from my forehead and into my face. The sky hung there reddish blue, no longer firmly anchored, and the river was spooling brown eddies of water. I started to run before he registered that I was still alive. I never wanted to stop again. The terror came jolting up into my mouth, giving me the hiccups. A man wheeled his bike past me, ringing the bell, and called out:

Hey, sweetie, keep your mouth closed or else your heart'll catch a chill.

Reeling, I stopped in my tracks, my legs shaking, my hands heavy. I was burning and freezing and hadn't run far at all, just a short distance, but I felt as though I'd raced halfway around the globe. I could still feel his viselike grip cutting into my neck. The man wheeled his bike into the park, the tires left long ripples snaking through the sand behind him, the tarmac ahead was completely deserted. The park was a sheer wall of blackish green, the sky clutching at the trees. The bridge made me horribly anxious and I couldn't help looking back. And there stood the suitcase, right in the middle of the bridge, exactly where it had been left. And he was standing right on the spot where I had run away from death, his face turned to the water. Between hiccups I could hear him whistling. Very melodically, without missing a beat, a tune he had learned from me. My hiccups vanished, frozen between one wave of terror and the next. I raised a hand to my throat and felt my larynx bobbing. Everything happened in a twinkling, the time it takes for one person to assault another. And there he stood on the bridge, whistling

> O the tree has its leaves,
> the tea has its water,
> money has its paper,
> and my heart has snow that's fallen astray.

Now I think it was a lucky thing that he grabbed me by the neck. That way no one could accuse me of provoking him. But he came very close to committing murder. All because he wasn't up to giving me a good beating, and because he despised himself for that.

The father had nodded off and was holding the child so loosely I could see him falling any moment. Then the boy kicked him in the stomach with his shoes. The father gave a start and pulled the boy back onto his lap. The boy's little sandals are dangling like little toys, as if his parents had dressed him that morning in some of his playthings. Their new soles had yet to step on the street. The father has handed the boy a handkerchief to play with. It's knotted, and must have a hard object wrapped into the knot, which the child is now using to hit the windowpane. Coins maybe, keys, nails, or else screws the father doesn't want to lose. The driver hears the banging; he turns around and says: Go on, keep it up, those windows cost money, you know. Don't worry, says the father, we're not going to break it. He taps on the pane and points outside and says to the boy: See that, there's a baby inside there who's even smaller than you. The boy drops the handkerchief and says: Mami. He sees a woman with a stroller. And the father says: Our Mami doesn't wear sunglasses. If she did, she wouldn't be able to see how blue your eyes are.

Whenever Paul asks me about my first husband, I say:

I've forgotten all that, I don't remember a thing.

I think I have more secrets from Paul than he does from me. Lilli once said that secrets don't go away when you tell them, what you can tell are the shells, not the kernel. That may have been true for her, but for me, if I don't keep something concealed, then I've already exposed the kernel.

You call it shells, I said, when something goes as far as it did on the bridge.

But you tell the story the way it suits you, Lilli said.

How is it supposed to suit me, it doesn't suit me at all.

Of course it makes you look bad, and him as well, Lilli said, but it suits you because you can talk about it however you like.

Not however I like. I tell it the way it was. You just don't

32

believe I'm telling you anything you wouldn't tell me. That's why you're going on about shells.

The point is that no matter how often I tell these stories, they stay the same, like the secret about my stepfather.

The last thing I need is to drive myself crazy wondering about the alcoholic by the trash cans. And who knows what he's thinking; after all, he's been seeing me next to the window for days on end as well. Finally, since we've never managed to agree about the alcoholic, Paul and I have given up puzzling about the people down below. Whether they move in a square or in circles or straight ahead, it's impossible to know them. Even if you go down to the street and walk right next to them, what can you tell. The fact that their gait looks alien, as if their toes were in back, has nothing to do with their feet, only with me. Of course we're still constantly looking out our window. And even though there's nothing puzzling about a car parked, to no apparent purpose, behind the shops, or else perched halfway on the sidewalk in front of our apartment house, where no normal person is allowed to park—this is more than enough to keep us busy.

I prefer looking out the kitchen window. There the swallows fly through a vast stretch of sky in circles of their own invention. This morning they were flying low, and I chewed my walnut and could tell by looking at them that it was a whole new day. Since I've been summoned, it will have to stay a window day, even if I can see half a tree to one side of the Major's table. The tree must have grown the length of an arm since my first interrogation. In winter it's the bare wood that marks the time, in summer it's the foliage. The leaves nod or shake their head, depending on the wind, but I can't rely on that. When the question is short, it means Albu wants the answer right away. Short questions aren't necessarily the easiest.

I'll have to think about it.

You mean you'll have to think up some lie, he says. Of course you could have one all ready and waiting, but that takes brains. Which you don't have, sad to say.

All right, so I'm dumb, but not so dumb as to say something that might hurt me. Nor am I dumb enough to let myself feel pressured when Albu's trying to gauge if I'm lying or telling the truth. Sometimes his eyes are cool, sometimes they burn into me so that . . .

Sometimes Lilli is inside me and gazes too long into Albu's eyes.

I shuffle my shoes under the table, then it's not so quiet.

O the tree has its leaves,
the tea has its water,
money has its paper,
and my heart has snow that's fallen astray.

A winter and summer song, but for outside. In here you can quickly fall into a trap with foliage and snow. I don't know the tree's name, otherwise I'd sing ash, acacia, poplar in my head, and not just tree. I twist at the button on the blouse that grows. I never get as close to the branches as the Major, not from my small table. We both look at the tree at the same time. I would like to ask:

What sort of tree is that.

It would be a distraction. He wouldn't answer me, that's for sure, just scrape his chair forward and, with his trouser cuffs loose about his ankles, he might fiddle with his signet ring or play with the stub of his pencil and turn the question around:

Why do you need to know that.

What could I say then. He doesn't know why I always wear the same blouse, just as he always wears his signet ring. He also doesn't know why I twist the large button. And I don't know why he always keeps that chewed pencil stub, no longer than a match, lying on his table. Men wear signet rings, women wear earrings. Wedding rings make you superstitious, you never take them off until you die. If the man dies, the widow takes his ring and wears it next to hers, day and night, on her ring finger. Like all married people, Albu wears his narrow wedding ring at work. But jewelry at a job like that, tormenting people. It's not an ugly ring by any means, and if it weren't his it would be beautiful. The same is true of his eyes, cheeks, earlobes. I'm sure Lilli would gladly have stretched out her hands to stroke him; maybe even have introduced him to me one day as her lover.

He's good-looking, I'd have had to say.

Lilli's beauty was a given, what your eyes saw wasn't to blame for dazzling them so. Her nose, the curve of her neck, her ear, her knee, in your amazement you wanted to protect them, cover them with your hand, you were afraid for them, and your thoughts turned to death. But it never occurred to me that such skin might someday wrinkle. Between her being young and being dead, it never crossed my mind that Lilli might age. With Albu's skin, age is simply there, as if his flesh had nothing to do with it. His age is a rank to which he has been promoted in recognition of his sterling work. From this point on, nothing more will change, he will maintain his superiority, with nothing else to come but death. I wish it would come soon. Albu's good looks are flawless, tailor-made for interrogations, his personal appearance is never at risk, not even when he's slobbering on my hand. Perhaps it is his very distinction that forbids him to mention Lilli. The chewed pencil on his table doesn't suit him, or anyone else his age. Surely Albu doesn't need to save on pencils. Perhaps he's proud that his grandson is teething. A photo of his grandson might serve instead of the pencil stub, except that here, as in all offices, it's probably forbidden to put family pictures on display. Perhaps a stub like that works well for his upright script. Or maybe a longer pencil would rub at his signet ring. Or maybe the stub is supposed to let me know exactly how much is being written about people like me. We know everything, Albu says. Maybe so—and here I agree with Lilli—about the shells of the dead. But nothing about their secrets, nothing about the kernels, about Lilli, whom Albu never mentions. Nothing about good fortune or common sense, which together may cause something tomorrow that I cannot foresee today. And nothing about what chance may bring the day after tomorrow; after all, I am alive . . .

There's nothing special about the fact that Albu and I are looking at the tree together. Our eyes fall on other things at the same time as well: my table or his, a section of wall, the door, or the floor. Or he looks at his pencil and I look at my finger. Or he looks at his ring and I look at my large button. Or he looks at my face and I look at the wall. Or I look at his face and he looks at the door. Constantly looking each other in the face is tiring, particularly for me. The only things I trust here are the ones that don't change. But the tree is growing: it gave the blouse its name. I may leave my happiness at home, but the blouse that grows is here.

If I haven't been summoned, I go into town on foot, taking side streets as far as the Korso. Beneath the acacias it's raining either white flowers or yellow leaves. Or if nothing is falling, then the wind is rushing down. When I was still going to the factory, I rarely made it into town during the middle of the day—not more than twice a year. I had no idea so many people weren't at work at that hour. Unlike me, they are all paid to run around, having made up stories of burst pipes, illness, or funerals to tell the boss, and even bask in the sympathy of their colleagues and superiors before setting off on their outing. Just once I had my grandfather die because I wanted to buy a pair of gray platform shoes when the shops opened at nine on the dot. I'd seen them in the window late the previous afternoon. I lied, went into town, bought the shoes, and then the lie came true. Four days later at dinner my grandfather fell from his chair, dead. When the telegram arrived early the next morning, I took my three-day-old gray platforms and held them under the tap to make them swell. I put them on, went to the office and said I'd need the next two days off since my kitchen was flooded. Whenever I tell a bad lie, it comes true. I took the train to attend the funeral. My shoes dried on my feet from one station to the next; I got out at the eleventh. The whole world was upside down, I carried the funeral from my lie all the way to that little town and then found myself standing in the cemetery facing the flood in the kitchen. The thump of the clods falling on the coffin lid sounded like my gray shoes on the path as I followed the procession.

In those days I was a good liar. Nobody ever found me out. But the trouble was that the lies themselves began to take me at my word. Since then I've preferred to be caught in a lie rather than be caught by trouble. The exception is Albu—there I'm good at lying.

These days I walk aimlessly into town. Riding to the factory never seemed to make any sense. It's hard to believe, but the senselessness kept itself better concealed in those days. If I sit down at a sidewalk café and order an ice cream, as I did yesterday,

I immediately decide I want a piece of cake. In reality all I want is to sit: not even that, just stop walking for a while. Making myself comfortable, I push the chair closer to the table. Once the chair is right, I want to jump up and leave, but I'm still not ready to go on walking. From far away the streetside tables are a destination, inviting me to linger, the tablecloth corners fluttering. Only when I'm sitting comfortably does my impatience flare up. Just when my exasperation at the wait reaches the breaking point, the ice cream arrives. The table is round, so is the ice cream dish, so are the scoops of ice cream. Next come the wasps. They're very pushy and determined to eat their fill, their heads are also round. Although I had to think twice before spending any money, I can't bear to eat what I've just paid for.

Senselessness was easier for me to handle than aimlessness. Nowadays I invent goals to pursue around town instead of lies in the factory. I follow women my age. I spend hours in the clothing stores and try on the things they like. Only yesterday I put on a striped dress, deliberately backward. I plucked and pulled at it, placed my hands around the neckline as a collar, and let my fingers dangle as if they were a bow. I was beginning to like the dress. What I hadn't reckoned with was this feeling of leaving myself behind. The dress looked as if I'd have to say goodbye quickly. My mouth was bitter, I couldn't think of anything to say to myself in the short time I had left. I didn't want to sit back and just let myself disappear, and I said:

Why now of all times, you won't get far without my feet.

I said it out loud, my face turning red. I don't want to be one of those people who look like lunatics because they're talking to themselves out loud. Some people sing. I don't want someone near me to shake his head because I can't tell thinking from speaking. Having total strangers hear what you're saying makes an even greater fool of you than if they don't see you at all and barge right into you. Although she must have heard me, one woman for whom I obviously didn't exist opened the curtain to my changing room, rudely set her bag on the chair, and asked:

Is this one taken.

Can't you see it is, after all you're speaking to me, not to an empty dressing room.

In the commotion I lost sight of the woman I had been following. I continued trying on clothes in the hope of becoming so beautiful I would begin to exist. Actually I'm not going to find anything, least of all myself, in the clothes other women want to buy. The clothes punish me; if another woman and I happen to try on the same outfit, I wind up all the more ugly by comparison. In the factory I tried on the most gorgeous dresses and strutted like a peacock, crossing the packing hall all the way to the door and back. When clothes were sewn for the West, I'd go upstairs with Lilli before the consignment was shipped. I'd try on two or three styles, one after the other.

That's enough, Lilli would say.

Because it was strictly forbidden. Not as strictly with skirts, trousers, and jackets as with blouses and dresses. We were allowed to buy dresses from the factory just before International Labor Day on the first of May and again in August before the Day of Liberation from the Yoke of Fascism. The office people bought the most. The dresses made for the West are more elegant and no more expensive than those in the shops. Unfortunately they're also full of weaving flaws and oil stains from the sewing machines, otherwise they'd be too good for the likes of us. Many people bought them by the sack: better weaving flaws and oil stains that never come out than the low-grade, mousy clothes in the state-owned stores. But I couldn't stand the weaving flaws and stains, and on top of everything else, I knew how attractive the dresses were that we weren't allowed to buy. The ones that wind up looking so nice on Italian, Canadian, Swedish, and French women, different ones for every season of their easygoing lives. Cutting, stitching, finishing, ironing, packing, and knowing all the time that you're not worthy of the final product. No doubt a lot of women thought:

Better a few coarse weaving flaws and black oil stains than nothing.

Because of the flaws and stains, and because I didn't want to have the factory at home in my wardrobe after spending the entire day there, I refused to buy the dresses. Sundays walking through the park wearing the factory rejects, eating ice cream in the café. The envious looks those dresses get you. You stand out. Everyone knows where you work, where you got them.

When Lilli and I went to the Korso after work and I went into the shops instead of continuing our walk, she would wait outside. I didn't have to hurry, Lilli disapproved if I came back too quickly. She'd stand with her back to the shop window and look at the sky, trees, asphalt, at the old men too, no doubt. I'd have to tug at her arm as if I'd been the one waiting for her, not the other way around. I'd say:

Come on, let's go.

What's the rush, she'd ask, aren't we going for a walk.

We can walk slowly, but let's just get away from here.

Didn't you like the clothes.

What is it you like so much about standing here.

She clicked her tongue.

Soft steps and a slightly stooped back, that's what I like.

And so.

So what.

How many have you seen, I'd ask.

Her lack of interest in shops had nothing to do with the factory. Even before, Lilli never had any time for clothes. Still, men would turn around to look at Lilli. I'd have noticed her too, if I had been a man. The worse she dressed, the more striking her beauty. It was all right for her, but I'd been vain since I was a child. When I was five I cried because my new coat was too big for me. My grandfather said:

You'll grow into it, wear some heavy clothes underneath, then it'll fit. In the old days, two or maybe three coats would have to last your entire life, if you were lucky, and that was if you were rich.

I'd put it on because I had to. But as soon as I'd turned the corner by the bread factory, I'd take it off. For two winters I carried it more than I wore it, I preferred being cold to looking ugly. And two snows later, when the coat finally fitted me, I refused to wear it because it was now too old as well as ugly.

If I were going to my hairdresser's, I'd have to get off right here, next to the student dormitories. I'd much prefer having my hair permed today, or even styled in a bun the way the old secretaries wear it. In fact, I'd rather be having my head shorn beyond recognition at ten sharp than be knocking on Albu's door. Than lose my wits while he kisses my hand. A beam of sunlight is beating down on the driver's cheek, the window next to him is open, but there's no wind coming through. He brushes the grains of salt off the console but doesn't touch his second crescent roll. Why buy three if all he needs is one. Leaving the tram to sit there, dashing off to the shops, then coming back and putting on this hunger act for all the people he's kept waiting. The child has fallen asleep, clutching the handkerchief. The father is resting his head against the window, and

41

although his hair is matted and dull from days without washing, the sun has set it aglow. Can't he feel that the tram's windowpane is even hotter than the sun outside. For the moment I'm safe in the shade, until we reach the bend in the tracks, and even then there's a chance the sun will keep to the other side of the car. I don't want to show up at Albu's dripping with sweat. I'm not sure I'd go so far as to switch seats, with so few passengers I'd get stared at. You need a reason. The father could move to the shady side anytime he wants, a small child counts as a reason. The father could change seats if the boy started to cry, in case it was because of the sun. On the other hand, if the tram were full he couldn't possibly do that, he'd be lucky to find a seat at all. No matter how much the child cried, the passengers wouldn't think about the sun, they'd just ask that fool of a father if he didn't have a pacifier for his miserable bawling brat.

What I used to like most about summer was playing with the son of the gatekeeper at the bread factory. We'd go to a path that ran alongside the broad avenue and was shaded by the same tall trees. The path was full of ruts and holes; we'd find the places where the dust was thickest. The boy was lame from birth, he would drag along behind me. We'd sit inside the deepest pothole, he'd bend his right leg and stiffly stretch his thin left one out in front. He was glad to be sitting down. He had nimble hands, curly hair, and a sallow complexion. We would become completely absorbed in our game, swirling the dust into snakes that went slithering all over one another.

That's how blindworms crawl through the flour, he said, that's why bread has holes.

No, the holes are because of the yeast.

They're because of the snakes, you can ask my father.

42

The snakes could have easily gone on slithering through the pothole for half the day, until his father came to fetch him, carrying a bag from the bread factory. But as soon as my dress got dirty I'd feel bad, so I would run home and leave the boy to fend off the blindworms on his own.

One day a different gatekeeper was keeping watch at the entrance to the bread factory. Two weeks later the boy's father returned, but without the boy. They had operated on that stiff leg and given the boy too much anesthetic. He never woke up. I would go to the path full of ruts and holes, where the trees stood huddled together casting their shade all the way to the avenue. I would keep to myself, avoiding the other children, as if the trees had promised that the boy would be coming here to play, even though he had died. I would sit down in the dirt and swirl up a snake, as thin and long as his stretched-out leg. The scraggly grass along the path. The tears dripping from my chin, forming a pattern on the snake. They'd taken the boy away from me, maybe he was looking down from heaven, maybe he realized that now I really did want to go on playing.

Lately when I go walking around town in the mornings it's Lilli I miss. She's the one they've taken away from me now.

The days when I'm summoned seem very short. Albu always has something in mind, even if I don't know exactly what he wants from me. All I need is the large button on my blouse and a clever lie. Of course when I'm wandering around town, I don't know exactly what I want from myself—even less than I know what Albu wants from me.

A little before eight this morning I watched the swallows: sometimes I think they're really driving or swimming instead of flying. That was a dumb thing to do, with Albu expecting me at ten sharp. I don't want to think about swallows. I don't want to think about anything at all, there's nothing to think about, because I myself am nothing, apart from being summoned. Last summer Paul still had his red motorbike, a Czech Java. Once or twice a week we'd go for a ride out of town, to the river. The lane through the beanfields—now that was happiness, good fortune, luck. The bigger the sky grew overhead, the more light-headed I felt. Whole jumbles of red flowers on each side, quivering as we flew past. You couldn't exactly see that every single flower had two round ears and open lips, but I knew it all the same. The beans went on forever, but not in visible rows like cornfields. Even after all the stalks have dried out and the wind has tattered the leaves, a late-summer cornfield always looks like it's just been combed. I never get light-headed in cornfields, even when the sky starts flying. Only a beanfield could strike me dumb with happiness, so much that I kept having to close my eyes from time to time. When I'd open them a moment later, I found I'd already missed a lot: the swallows were long since soaring in new orbits.

I held on tight to Paul's ribs and whistled the song about leaves and snow. I couldn't hear myself over the motorcycle. Usually I never whistle, because you have to have learned that as a child, and I never did. In fact, I still don't know how. And ever since my first husband whistled on the bridge, I flinch whenever I hear someone whistle. But in the beanfields it was me who was whistling. So it must have been luck, a bit of good fortune, because nothing else I do comes out half as well as my whistling in the beanfield. Surrounded by string beans, I was literally struck dumb with happiness. With the river it's different, the river never brings me happiness, though the smooth water always works to calm me down even when my thoughts stray to the bridge. But you can't find happiness in being calm. By the time we reached the riverbank, I was ill at ease and Paul was impatient. He was looking forward to the river, I was looking forward to the ride back through the beans. He stepped into the water up to his ankles and showed me a black dragonfly, its abdomen hanging between its wings like a spiral made of glass. I pointed out the glossy dark clusters of blackberries beside me on the bank. And across the river the black starlings were settling onto pale rectangular bales of straw in a field of stubble. But I didn't point those out, because I was looking at the sky, focusing on the little flecks of swallows, unable to understand how the color black is doled out and shared with the scorched yellow of a summer day. I laughed in my befuddlement, picked up a piece of tree bark from the grass, and threw it right at Paul's feet. Then I said: You know, those swallows can't really fly as fast as it seems, they're just trying to trick us.

Paul fished for the bark with his toes and pushed it under the water. When he removed his foot, the wood bobbed right back up, shiny and black. He said:

Um-hmm.

He glanced up just long enough for me to see the dark daubs inside his eyes. Why ask what black fruit he has lurking in his eyes if he won't even talk about the swallows and if his thoughts are so far removed from his toes. A breeze was rustling in the ash trees, I listened to the leaves, perhaps Paul was listening to the water. But he didn't want to talk.

The next day in the factory I tried using the Um-hmm on Nelu when he came to my desk, pinching a sheet of paper between his thumb and coffee cup. He started rambling about button sizes for the ladies' coats we were making for France that month. The tips of his mustache flapped around his mouth like swallow wings. I let him speak several sentences right into my face. When he came to the weekly schedule, I counted how many chin hairs he had missed while shaving. I raised my eyes

45

and sought his. As soon as our pupils met I came right out with it:

Um-hmm.

Nelu was silent and walked over to his desk. I also tried out other words, such as Ah and Oh. But nothing could beat Um-hmm.

When I was confronted about the notes, he denied having informed on me. Anyone can deny things. It was just after I had separated from my first husband; white linen suits were being packed up for Italy. After we went on a ten-day business trip together, Nelu expected to keep on sleeping with me. But I'd made up my mind to marry a Westerner, and I slipped the same note into ten back pockets: Marry me, *ti aspetto,* signed with my name and address. The first Italian who replied would be accepted.

At the meeting, which I was not allowed to attend, my notes were judged to be prostitution in the workplace. Lilli told me Nelu had argued for treason, but had failed to convince them. Since I wasn't a Party member and since it was my first offense, they decided to give me a chance to mend my ways. I wasn't fired, which was a defeat for Nelu. The man in charge of ideological affairs personally delivered two written reprimands to my office. I had to sign the original for the records, the copy remained on my desk.

I'll frame it, I said.

Nelu didn't see what there was to joke about. He sat on his chair, sharpening a pencil.

What do you want with the Italians, they'll come and screw you, give you pantyhose and a little deodorant, then go back home to their fountains. For a blowjob they'll throw in some perfume.

I watched the frilly wood peelings and the black powder

46

spilling out of his sharpener and stood up. I held the reprimand over his head and let go. The sheet floated down and settled on the table in front of him without a sound. Nelu turned his head toward me and tried to smile, pale as a worm. Then he accidentally nudged the newly sharpened pencil with his elbow. We watched it roll off the table, and listened to it chime against the floor. Nelu bent down so that I could no longer see how tensely he was working his jaws. The pencil tip had broken off. He said:

So what. A pencil fell on the floor, it's not like something exploded.

Who knows, I said. With someone like you, anything's possible.

That was my first day back in the factory after three days of questioning. Nelu didn't say another word to me. Evidently he was capable of worse than I had imagined. The three notes later found in trousers destined for Sweden read: Best wishes from the dictatorship. The notes were just like mine, but I didn't write them. I was fired.

Even if the snow was deep, we drove to work on the Java. Paul had ridden a motorbike for eleven years and never had an accident, despite the fact that he drank. He knew the streets like the back of his hand and could have found both our factories with his eyes closed. I was all wrapped up, the streetlamps and lighted windows were glittering, the frost bit into our faces, our lips felt like frozen crusts of bread, our cheeks as smooth and cold as porcelain. Sky and street were nothing but snow, we were driving into a great big snowball. I leaned against Paul's back and pressed my chin against his shoulder to let the snowball flow through my face. The streets are longest, the trees tallest, the sky closest when your eyes are fixed straight ahead. I wanted to go on riding and never stop. I didn't dare

47

blink. My ears were burning, my fingers, toes. The frost scorched me like an iron, only my eyes and mouth stayed cold. There was no time for luck or good fortune, we had to get there before we froze, and every morning we pulled up to my factory gate at half past six on the dot. Paul let me off. Using one reddish-blue finger to push up his cap, I kissed his porcelain forehead, then pulled the cap back down over his eyebrows. Afterwards he drove off to the engine works on the edge of town. When I saw hoarfrost on his eyebrows, I thought:

Now we are old.

After the business with the first notes, I put Italy out of my mind completely. It took more than linen suits for export to land a Marcello, you needed connections, couriers, and intermediaries, not trouser pockets. Instead of an Italian I landed the Major. My stupidity screamed at me, my self-reproach was sharp as a blow to the ears. I felt I was stuffed with straw. I couldn't abide myself: that was the only way I could carry on every day, sitting in the office with Nelu, staring at columns and filling them in, until the second notes turned up. But I still liked myself: that was why I could enjoy riding the trams, having my hair cut short, buying new clothes. I also felt sorry for myself: that was why I could make it to Albu's at precisely the right time. I felt indifferent toward myself too, as though the interrogations were a just punishment for my stupidity. But not for the reasons Albu cited:

Your behavior makes foreigners think all our countrywomen are whores.

I don't see how, the notes never made it to Italy.

Thanks to the care shown by your colleagues, he said.

Why whores, anyway—I only wanted one Italian, and I wanted to marry him. Whores want money, not marriage.

The foundation of marriage is love and love alone. Do you

even know what that is. You wanted to sell yourself to the Marcellos like a filthy slut.

Why like a filthy slut, I would have loved him.

It was over, I was back outside, back in the summer brightness, with everyone going about his noisy business. I could hear the straw rustling inside me. Chances are I wouldn't have loved the Italian, but he would have taken me with him to Italy. I would have tried to love him. If I couldn't, I would have found somebody else, after all, there's no shortage of Italians in Italy. There's always someone you can love if you put your mind to it. But instead of love I wound up with Albu summoning me as often as he pleased. And Nelu keeping a close watch on me at work. I put men completely out of my mind. Then I got caught up in Paul, right when I was on the defensive. I think being on the defensive sharpens my desire, much more than being actively on the lookout for someone. It had to have been that way, that's why I clung to him so. It's not that anybody could have transformed my defensiveness into desire, although it's possible that someone other than Paul might have done so. Weary of life—that's how I must have felt, without a good hold on things. And then one Sunday I met Paul. I stayed through Monday, and on Tuesday I moved in with him, lugging all my worldly possessions into the leaning tower.

Each morning I found it harder and harder to go to work. Paul would grip his Java firmly in both hands outside the factory gate, smile, wait for me to kiss his forehead and say:

You have to act like Nelu isn't there.

Easy for him to say. But how to spend eight hours on end acting as if two mustache tips were simply floating in midair behind a desk.

Nelu's so full of it, I said, that you can't see through him.

And the motorbike roared, kicking up snow around the

wheels, or dust. When Paul was halfway down the street I tried coaxing him back to the gate with my eyes, each morning I wanted to say something more to him, something he could take to last him the whole day among the machines. But we always repeated the same words.

Paul: You have to act like Nelu isn't there.

Me: I'll be thinking of you. Don't get worked up if they steal your clothes.

The quick getaway. And the wind when he turned the corner, his jacket arching back like a cat ready to pounce. Every morning I had to force myself to step inside the factory. The mere sight of Nelu was enough to drive me crazy. Neither of us greeted the other, though after an hour or two Nelu would try to break the silence, claiming that we couldn't possibly stay in the same room together for eight hours at a stretch without saying something. I didn't feel the need to say anything, but he couldn't stand the silence. He talked about the production schedule, I said:

Um-hmm.

Um-hmm, and Oh, and Ah.

When that didn't work, I turned chatty. I picked up the little vase on his desk, peered through the thick glass on the bottom and studied the reddish-green rose stem inside the water. I said:

Come on now, why talk about the schedule when there's no point in meeting the targets. If we ever did, they'd be raised the next day. That schedule of yours is a disease of state.

Nelu plucked a hair from his mustache and rubbed it between his fingers so that it curled up. He said:

Do you like it.

If you pull out one a day, pretty soon your face will look like a cucumber, I said.

50

Don't get too excited. You're obviously thinking of pubic hair.

But not yours, I said.

Do you know why Italians always carry a comb in their pocket—because otherwise they can't find their pricks when they have to piss.

You've got a comb too, but even that won't help you. You don't have what it takes to be an Italian.

I've seen what it takes, unlike you I've been to Italy.

Um-hmm. And did you do a little spying there too, I asked.

It's true I was thinking of pubic hair, Nelu forced me to think of his all the time he was talking about the schedule. He placed that hair right in the middle of my desk, too, where there was a nick in the wood. Not one I had made. He'd probably gone and measured the desk to locate the spot furthest from my reach. I didn't want to touch that curly hair of his, but I didn't have my ruler handy to flick it off the table right then and there. So once again I wound up doing something he really enjoyed seeing, I blew the hair away. The sight of me pursing my lips gave him something to laugh at. I had to blow three or four times before the hair flew off the table. He made me obscene.

One day the cleaning lady will come into the office after work and she'll be wiping away blood instead of dust, I said to Lilli. It won't be long now. One of these days I'm going to lose control and kill the son of a bitch.

Lilli brushed me off with a wave of her hand and said:

Don't you dare. Why not just leave a knife on his desk and tell him how good it would feel against his throat, that it doesn't hurt at all. Then move away a little, like on the bridge, so he won't feel awkward. He's doing everything he can to make you lose control, and you're letting him, you're positively asking for it. Keep a hold on yourself and you won't lose your grip. It just takes practice.

Lilli's plum-blue eyes met my own and her gaze won. And her smooth neck. I knew from the bridge how fast you can lose your grip, how quickly you can send another person to his death when he starts to weigh on you, like stones piled on your heart. And I knew this would happen again, with Nelu.

Lilli dismissed me with a wave of her hand, then blushed. Her nose was twitching, but it stayed cool and white. At that moment I hated everything about Lilli, as she stood there before me, but even so I couldn't help thinking:

That nose is as beautiful as a tobacco flower.

Lilli considered me an instigator. I had frightened her, and now she was using the bridge against me. I could see signs of hate lurking in her features; I wish I'd never found out how much that made her look like her mother. At the funeral you could hear the earth ringing on the coffin, then it closed over Lilli, and that mother of hers snapped at me, with Lilli's mouth.

That's right, keep a hold on yourself—Lilli thought—it just takes practice. She could see the threads running through my tangled thoughts more clearly than I could. And I imagined I could see through her own tangle more clearly than she did. There was a time when we could have swapped places, she and I. Instead, she traded with her mother. Keep a hold on yourself, she thought, and you'll make it across the border. Don't lose your grip, the bullets only hit you if you let them know you're worried. It just takes practice, and she wanted to learn. Back when she told me to keep a hold on myself with Nelu, Lilli was just starting to sleep with a sixty-six-year-old officer. A couple of weeks later they decided to flee across the Hungarian border.

He was arrested and she was shot dead. Too clever for her own good, Lilli.

Once she took me to the summer garden of the officers' mess and introduced me to her officer. He was wearing civilian clothes, a short-sleeved shirt with narrow stripes and light-weight gray trousers that reached high up under his arms. He had no ribs and no hips. In his deep, quiet voice he said: It's a pleasure to meet you, miss.

He kissed my hand. A finely practiced kiss from the old royal age, dry and light and in the middle of my hand. Young men in uniform were sitting at the surrounding tables. Naturally Lilli attracted their attention, the uniformed men were mad about beautiful women, they threw match heads at Lilli. They figured out that she was the officer's skirt, not me.

It had been a long time since the last war. Idleness threatened to erode military discipline, which had to be shored up with so-called precision work, namely, the conquest of beautiful women. Beauty was graded according to the face, the curve of the backside, the shapeliness of the calves seen together, and the breasts. The breasts were dubbed apples, pears, or windfall peaches, depending on the position of the nipples. The conquest of women has taken the place of maneuvers, the soldiers were told. Everything between her neck and thighs has to be just right. The legs and face aren't so important: once you've got her legs apart and you're going at it, you can always shut your eyes if you don't want to look at her face. With breasts, though, it's a different matter. Apples are good, pears are okay, but windfalls are always overripe and beneath consideration for soldiers. Each conquest, so they said, keeps your body's joints oiled and helps maintain your inner balance. And that improves the harmony of your marriage. The old officer had thoroughly educated Lilli about the best tactics for combating idleness in peacetime. He too had been on constant maneuvers, Lilli said, until his wife died. She was fifty and he was six years older. After she died he no longer had to pretend that the satisfying work that produced his sweet weariness was done in the field rather than other women's beds. He visited the cemetery every day; chasing after women now seemed stale.

All the women I knew suddenly sounded like cackling hens and tasted like sour fruit, he said, especially the very young ones. Life became a mincing parade of calves drawn taut by stiletto heels marching across the asphalt, from the barracks to the officers' mess and back. Between the sheets the women were all barefoot, moist, and groaning. Any moment was as good as another for dying, he was afraid they might do it underneath him.

Taken each on his own, every uniformed man in that summer garden was a loser, even with the pears and the windfalls. And Lilli had small firm summer apples. After only a few words Lilli would have sent any one of them packing. They guessed as much, which was why they practiced the conquest of Lilli together, as a regimental exercise. In their view, Lilli's officer no longer needed to oil his joints, he was past precision work, it was time he was relieved. They pressured him to give others a go at Lilli's gorgeous flesh. As they tossed one match head after the other, the wedding rings they wore on their fingers glinted in the sun, while their eyes, fixed on their target, flashed like greased bullets. The old man set the ashtray next to his hand and said:

They're sick. We should have gone somewhere else.

He gathered the match heads from the table and tossed them into the ashtray. His hands were as white and slender as a pharmacist's. Neither he nor Lilli made a move to get up. They weren't pretending to be calm; they were merely being patient. I couldn't understand it, you only have that kind of patience if you know you won't need it long. The officer's temples were pulsing, but his face was still smooth, dappled beneath the sunshade like blotchy paper. The way Lilli looked at him, utterly without reserve, was new to me. Her gaze and his—like plums falling into still water. When he leaned in to take Lilli's hand, his belly slid forward like a ball. Another two matches landed on the table. Now he'll get angry, I thought. But he merely gathered these as well, using his free hand, while he was so sure of Lilli's hand that he suddenly started to sing to her, softly:

A horse is coming into camp
with a window in its head.
Do you see the tower looming high and blue . . .

The fact that he'd sing at all, so deep, although without revealing anything of his inner self, was moving enough. But the idea that he knew the song in the first place cut me to the quick. My grandfather used to sing the same song; he had learned it in the camp. The officer was obviously counting on Lilli and me being too young to know it. My God, it would have tied his tongue if I had joined in. As it was, the song sounded awkward, here at the table, simply because I was sitting between them, listening. I looked up and saw where the umbrella fabric had worn through at the spokes. We ourselves were caught in the spokes of a great wheel, and I was violating a secret. For the officer, Lilli wasn't just another pleasant pastime, he loved her. And when he stopped singing, I left Lilli sitting beside him in the officers' mess and went walking through town in a daze. Already then they must have been thinking about getting out. He had two grown-up sons in Canada, that's where he wanted to take her.

The sun was beating down, the leaves fluttered green and yellow in the linden trees, but only the yellow ones drifted to the ground. However I looked at it, green stood for Lilli and yellow for him.

This man's too old for Lilli.

I bumped into other pedestrians, didn't see them in time. That afternoon I was utterly alone, and remained so until the next morning in the factory when Lilli called me over to talk about the officer.

Since the business with the notes I was no longer allowed in the packing hall. Lilli was waiting in the corridor as I climbed the stairs. We went to a corner in the back, she squatted on her heels, I leaned my shoulder against the wall and said:

His face is young, but his stomach's round as a ball, like the setting sun.

At this Lilli stiffened, anchored her fingertips on the floor, and opened her eyes wide. I had hurt her feelings. A vein swelled inside her throat, her mouth hardened as if she were going to shout. But Lilli took my hand and pulled me down to her, so that I too was crouching, holding on to her hip. A man with an armload of coat hangers came shuffling past, pretending not to see us. Lilli whispered:

When he lies down, the setting sun goes flat as a pillow.

I was looking at Lilli's feet. When the second toe's longer than the big toe, they call it a widow's toe. Lilli's was like that. She said:

He calls me Cherry.

The name didn't fit her blue eyes. The man with the coat hangers was moving further and further away. After he closed the door of the packing hall behind him, Lilli said:

The wind plucks cherries off the branch. Isn't it great: you're the one with such dark eyes and I'm the one he calls Cherry.

Sunlight fell in the corridor, while fluorescent lights were burning overhead. We were two tired children, sitting there like that.

Was he in a camp, I asked.

Lilli didn't know.

Will you ask him.

Lilli nodded.

Strange, not a single sound came from the factory yard, and in the corridor it was so still you could hear the crackle of the fluorescent lights.

Now I believe the old officer needed to search out Lilli because he'd already come to terms with her death—even before he met her. That when he first saw her he halted like a stopwatch and said: This is the one for me. Despite the fact that he was retired, he was still drawn to the officers' mess, to the uniforms—though his own had been laid aside, it had melded with his skin. Deep down he wanted to remain a soldier. He wanted to take Lilli where people would see him in the uniform he had once worn, despite the short-sleeved shirt with narrow stripes he now had on. To show off his conquest in the soldiers' garden, and, when he was alone with Lilli, to work his late craving for love to a fervor that outdid Lilli's beauty. A man of his kind knew plenty about soldiers, dogs, and bullets at the border. But his fear that Death might desire Lilli as greatly as he did yielded to the conviction that Lilli could look Death in the eye and stare Death down, both for his sake as well as her own. He saw too much, and was blinded. He risked Lilli, who meant more to him than reason can bear.

Everyone getting on in years thinks of times gone by. The

57

snot-nosed border guard who shot Lilli resembled the old officer in his own memories of youth. The guard was a young farmer, or a laborer. Maybe he began his studies a month or so afterward, and went on to become a teacher or doctor or priest or engineer. Who knows. When he fired, he was just a man on duty, a miserable sentry under a vast heaven where the wind whistled loneliness day and night. Lilli's living flesh gave him shivers, and her death was heaven-sent, an unexpected gift of ten days' leave. Perhaps he wrote unhappy letters like my first husband. Perhaps a woman like me was waiting, someone who, although she couldn't measure up to the dead woman, could nonetheless laugh and caress her man in the grip of love until he felt like a human being. Perhaps at that moment it was the thought of his good fortune that pulled the trigger, and then the shot rang out. From far away there was barking, followed by shouting. Lilli's officer was handcuffed, taken away to a tin hut, and guarded by the youth who had fired the shot, immersed in thoughts of his good fortune. Lilli lay where she had fallen. The hut was open at the front. On the floor was a water tank, a bench along the wall, in the corner a stretcher. The guard took a deep drink of water, washed his face, pulled his shirt out of his trousers, wiped himself dry, and sat down. The prisoner was not allowed to sit, although he was permitted to look over at the grass where Lilli lay. Five dogs came running, their legs flying over the grass, which was as high as their throats. Trailing far behind, a number of hard-driven soldiers ran after them. By the time they reached Lilli, it was not only her dress that was in tatters. The dogs had torn Lilli's body to shreds. Under their muzzles Lilli lay red as a bed of poppies. The soldiers drove off the dogs and stood around in a circle. Then two of them went to the hut, took a drink of water, and carried back the stretcher.

Lilli's stepfather told me this. Red as a bed of poppies, he said. And when he said it, I thought of cherries.

The boy has fallen asleep in the sun. The father tugs at the handkerchief, the fingers loosen, the boy goes on sleeping even while his father bends the little arm back so he can return the handkerchief to its jacket pocket. Even while the father stands up, spreads his legs, and turns the boy around so his back is facing forward and his open mouth is pressed against the father's shoulder. We're almost at the main post office. The father carries the child to the door of the car. The tram comes to a stop, the temporary silence makes the car seem even emptier. The driver reaches for the second crescent roll, then hesitates and takes a swig from his bottle. Why is he drinking before he eats. The giant blue mailbox is in front of the post office, how many letters can it take. If it were up to me to fill it, it would never have to be emptied. Since the notes meant for Italy, I haven't written to a soul—just told someone something now and then: you have to talk, but you don't have to write. The driver is munching away at his second roll, it must have dried out a little, judging by the crumbs. Outside, the father carries the sleeping boy across the middle of the street, where there isn't a safe crossing. If a car comes now he won't make it. How's he supposed to run carrying a child, and a sleeping child at that. Maybe he checked to make sure there was nothing coming before he crossed. But he'd have to look over the boy's head to see what might be coming from the right, and he could easily miss something. If there's an accident, it'll be his fault. This is the same man who, before the boy fell asleep, said: Our Mami doesn't wear sunglasses. If she did, she wouldn't see how blue your eyes are. He walks up to the post office, carrying the child like a parcel. If the boy doesn't wake up, he'll put him in the mail. An old woman sticks her head in the open door and asks: Does this tram go to the market. Why don't you read what's on the sign, the driver says. I'm not wearing my glasses, she says. Well, we just go and follow our nose and if that takes us to the market then we'll get there. The old woman gets in, and the driver starts up. A young man takes a running jump on board. He's panting so loud it takes my breath away.

I had spotted Lilli's stepfather at a table outside a café. He pretended not to recognize me, but I said good morning before he could turn his head away. That morning it had looked like rain, and many of the sidewalk tables were unoccupied. I sat down at his. It's all right to bother people sitting at sidewalk tables. He ordered a coffee and said nothing. I also ordered a coffee and said nothing. This time I had an umbrella crooked over my arm, and he was wearing a straw hat. He looked different than he had at Lilli's funeral. As he tossed shriveled acacia leaves from the tablecloth into the ashtray he looked more like Lilli's officer. But his hands were clumsy and ungainly. Once the waitress had set our coffees on the table, he put his thumb on the handle of his cup and turned it around and around on the saucer until it squeaked. Grains of sugar stuck to his thumb, he rubbed them off with his index finger, then lifted his cup and slurped.

This is so weak it's thinner than pantyhose, he said.

Was that supposed to make me think about his love in the kitchen. I said: It could be stronger.

At that he gave a brief laugh and raised his eyes as if he were resigned to my presence.

I'm sure Lilli told you that I used to be an officer too, but that's long ago now. I managed to visit Lilli's officer in prison. I didn't know him earlier, only his name, from years ago. Did you know him. — *m question meets for my question*

By sight, I said.

He had better luck than Lilli, he said, or maybe not, depending. Things look pretty bad for him.

He flattened a crumpled acacia leaf with his index finger, it tore down the middle, he threw it onto the ground, spluttered, coughed, cleared his throat, looked in the ashtray, and said:

It's almost fall.

That's something I can talk about with anyone, I thought, and said:

Pretty soon.

You asked at the funeral what Lilli looked like. Are you sure you want to know.

I gripped my cup so he couldn't see how my hand was shaking. More and more drops were falling onto the tablecloth, nevertheless he pulled his straw hat down over his eyes and went on:

The officer paid a fortune. A man with a motorbike and sidecar was supposed to be waiting on the Hungarian side. And he did wait, the week before, but only long enough to get his money; after that he didn't wait to go to the police and pick up another nice little bundle. Look over there, said Lilli's stepfather, it's clearing up again behind the park.

Lilli had loved a hotel porter, a doctor, a dealer in leather goods, a photographer. Old men, to my way of thinking, at least twenty years older than she was. She didn't call any of them old. She'd say:

He isn't exactly young.

But until the old officer, none of the men had ever come between Lilli and me, had ever caused me to feel one way or the

61

other. He was the only one who made her neglect me. It was the first time I'd been left to my own devices—as happened that day in the officers' mess—for an extended period. Here this man comes shuffling along, having already enjoyed the best years of his life, and snaps up Lilli. I was sad and jealous, but not in the obvious way. It wasn't the old man I envied, but Lilli for having him. I didn't find the old man the least bit attractive, but there was something about him that made you sorry for not liking him. Even sorry that he didn't care for you. Between the old officer and myself I felt regret, but it was regret about something I neither would have wanted nor allowed. He was a man who aroused no desire and who left you no peace. That's why I had to say his stomach was round as a ball, like the setting sun. The remark was directed at Lilli, not him. And that makes me, too, part of his coming to terms with her death.

Lilli liked old men, her stepfather was the first. She forced herself on him; she wanted to sleep with him and told him so. He kept her on tenterhooks, but she refused to give up. One day, when Lilli's mother had gone to the hairdresser's, Lilli asked him how much longer he was going to go on avoiding her. He sent her out to buy bread. There was no line in the shop: she got her bread and was back in no time.

Where do you want me to go now so you can get a grip on yourself, she asked.

And he asked in return whether she was sure she could keep so huge a secret.

Even a child has secrets, Lilli said to me, and I wasn't a child anymore. I put the loaf down on the kitchen table and pulled my dress over my head as if it were a handkerchief. That's how it all started. It went on for over two years, nearly every day except Sundays, and always in a rush, always in the kitchen, we never touched the beds. He'd send my mother to the shop, sometimes there'd be a long line, sometimes a short one, she never caught us.

Apart from me, only three others from the factory dared attend Lilli's funeral. Two girls from the packing department came of their own accord. The rest refused to have anything to do with an escape attempt and the way it had ended. The third person was Nelu, he came on orders. One of the two girls pointed out Lilli's stepfather to me. He was carrying a black umbrella on his arm. That day it didn't look like rain, the sky was soaring in a great blue arc, the flowers in the cemetery smelled of fresh breezes, not pungent and heavy the way they do before a rain. And the flies were flitting about the flowers, not buzzing around your head the way they do before a thunderstorm. I couldn't decide whether carrying an umbrella in that weather made a man look dignified or affected. One thing was certain, it made him look different. A little like an aimless idler, but also like a practiced scoundrel with crooked ways, who visits the cemetery at the same time every day and not for the peace it affords. Someone who might keep tabs on who shows up at this grave or that.

Nelu was carrying a small bunch of sweet peas, little ruffled white flowers. In his hands, snow on a stem was as wrong as the stepfather's black umbrella. I walked over to Lilli's stepfather without introducing myself. He guessed who I was.

You knew Lilli well.

I nodded. Maybe he could sense from the aura around my forehead that I was thinking of his kitchen love affair. He felt closer to me than I did to him, he leaned forward to be embraced. I remained stiff, and he straightened up again. His umbrella swung as he drew back, then he stretched his hand out as a greeting, keeping his arm bent. His hand was wooden and dry. I asked:

What did Lilli look like.

He forgot the umbrella and it slid down to his wrist. At the last moment he caught it with his thumb.

Inside that wooden coffin is another one made of zinc, he said. They welded it shut.

He merely raised his chin, keeping his eyes lowered, and whispered:

Look over there, the fourth from the right, that's Lilli's mother, go to her.

I went to the woman dressed in black, whom he had called Lilli's mother and not his wife—in keeping with his kitchen affair. She had shared him with Lilli for nearly three years. She quickly offered me one yellow cheek and then the other. I kissed them far to the side, halfway on her black headscarf. She, too, realized who I was:

You knew, didn't you. An officer, and he didn't know any better.

I was thinking of the kitchen. What was she thinking of. When the mourners filed past, Nelu threw his white sweet peas onto the coffin and a clod of earth after them. At the very least I wanted to knock the clod of earth from his hand before it hit the coffin. He nodded to me. I can't say what Lilli's mother felt at that moment.

Lilli might have listened to you. It's better if you go now.

Her hatred had slipped out into the open. He sends me over to her, and I go. She blames me and sends me packing, and again I go. What did the two of them think they were doing, why didn't I say:

64

Listen, I'll stay as long as I want.

A number of velvet shoes with embroidered leaf-patterns stood on the ground. They belonged to Lilli's relatives from the village. Their white stockings were soiled at the toes and at the heels. Behind them was Nelu. He whispered:

Psst, got a light.

He held the cigarette in his cupped hand, the filter peeping out under his thumb.

You're not supposed to smoke here, I said.

Why not, he asked.

You seem nervous.

Aren't you nervous.

No.

Come off it. These things get everybody all shaken up.

What things, I asked.

You know. Death.

I thought you were assigned to Italy. I didn't know Canada was in your department.

Are you crazy.

Tell me, how can you stand it all, the fresh earth and everything.

The exchange was fast, we were talking too loud. A walking stick rapped against my ankle, and an old man in velvet shoes said:

Good God Almighty, is nothing sacred. If you two want to quarrel, at least don't do it here.

My heart was thumping inside my head. I took a breath in order to change my tone, and said, as if I were sweetness and light itself:

We're sorry.

I walked off, leaving Nelu standing there. The earth had

still not settled on one of the other graves in Lilli's row. A new wooden cross and beside it a plate, smeared with food, and I simply couldn't believe that I had apologized for Nelu as well as myself.

You give the dead food to take on their way to heaven, to distract the evil spirits. On the first night, the soul sneaks around them, past hell, to God. Lilli's mother will give her a plate too. During the night, the cemetery cats will enjoy a feast on her rectangular mound of soil. The echo of my steps on the paved path was louder than the spadework at the grave. I held my hands to my ears and started running toward the gate. If I didn't want to understand Lilli's love for the old men, it was because . . .

A bus was waiting at the entrance to the cemetery gate. My father was sitting asleep at the wheel, with his face buried in his hands—despite the fact that he'd been dead for years. Since his death I had frequently spotted him sitting at the wheel of a moving bus or one that was parked. The reason he died was to get away from Mama and me; he wanted to go on driving undisturbed through the streets, without having to hide from us. And so he just keeled over right before our eyes and died. We shook him, his arms swung limply back and forth and then went rigid. His face drew taut against his cheekbones, his forehead felt like vinyl—cold, with a coldness that shouldn't occur in humans, it's too unforgettable. I kept caressing his brow and prying his eyes open so that they'd roll back around, so that the light would enter and force him to live. But every touch seemed indecent. I kept tugging at him while Mama turned away as if he'd never belonged to her at all. His keeling over showed us exactly how a person can shun help, how a person can simply decide to grow cold like that, with utter disregard for anyone else. From one moment to the next, he had unhitched

66

himself from Mama and me and left us to ourselves. Then the doctor arrived. He laid Papa on the couch and asked:

Where's the old man.

My grandfather is at his brother's in the country, I said, they don't have a telephone and the postman only comes once a week. He won't be back until the day after tomorrow.

The doctor wrote the word stroke on an official form, stamped it, signed it, and left. With his hand on the door, he said:

It's hard to believe—your husband was in great condition, but his brain just switched off, like a lightbulb.

A glass of sparkling water, which the doctor had requested but not drunk, was standing on the table, fizzing away. When he keeled over, Papa had brought the chair down with him. Now the backrest was lying on the floor and the seat was vertical. It was upholstered in a reddish-gray houndstooth check. Mama tiptoed into the kitchen with the glass of water, glancing back at the couch as if her husband were taking his afternoon nap. She didn't spill a single drop. From the kitchen came the one brief sound of a glass being set down. After that she came back into the room and sat down at the table where the glass had been. And then there were two people in that room who weren't fully alive and one who was dead. Three people who for years had been lying every time they referred to themselves as "we," or said "our" about a water glass, a chair, or a tree in the garden.

Since then, whenever I met my father in the streets, he seemed as unfamiliar as he did lying on the couch. I saw him everywhere, even at the entrance to the cemetery. All the buses throughout the country looked alike, they all had the same worn steps, the same rusty fenders, and at least half a year's accumulated dust on the roof, fine as flour. I peered in through the windows and suddenly saw the backrests of the vacant seats turn into passengers, and the windshield break out in little freckles, as Papa called the squashed bugs that dried in various shades of red and yellow. I saw women wearing white stockings and embroidered shoes and men with pinched faces and walking sticks—all Lilli's relations. Her father came from a valley in the hilly region, a mere wisp of a village, where the plum trees were drenched with blue and the branches sagged. The driver had to wait until Lilli was at last completely covered by earth. Lilli's soul would soon be in the care of the cemetery cats, but it would take half the night before the driver would return his farmers with their overtired faces safely to their plum trees.

While I was going to the girls' high school in our small town, and still living with my parents, I used to enjoy meeting my father for his last ride of the day, when he ran the empty bus back to the depot. In the near darkness of the streets, as the bus rattled along on its way, we felt no need to talk. The seats, the doors, the hand straps, the steps, every single part was loose, but somehow the bus as a whole held together. Every evening, after a long day's driving, Papa would tighten up the most important screws and tune the engine for the next morning. Riding to the depot, he would honk as he turned the corners and sail through the red lights. We would laugh when we had a close shave, when the lights of a truck passed within a hairsbreadth. As soon as we reached the depot he'd let me off at the big iron gates. I'd walk on and he'd take the bus inside, since he still had things to do. An hour and a half later he would show up at our house.

One evening a bug flew into my eye while I was walking home along the avenue. I stopped under a streetlamp, pulled down my lid and held it to my lashes. Then I blew my nose. It was a trick my grandfather had learned in the camp. I must have done it right, because when I was done the fly was caught in the corner of my eye, and I was able to wipe it away. But my eye was watering, and I needed a handkerchief. At that point I realized I'd left my bag in the bus. Papa wouldn't see it, he never thought of anything but the engine. So I turned back.

I entered the depot from the side. I knew my way well enough, but not in the dark, so I kept to the main building, where an ornate shaded lamp was burning beside the loading dock. I quickly found the bus. In the grass next to the front wheel I saw two empty wicker baskets. And inside the bus, on the seat next to the driver, I saw a braid of hair bouncing up and down. Then I made out cheeks, a nose, a throat. My dad was kissing the throat. He was sitting beneath a woman who was arching her head up as if she wanted to climb her own neck all the way to the ceiling. Her back was bent like a reed. I knew the woman, we had gone to the same girls' school. She had been in a different grade, but we were the same age. For the last three years she'd been selling vegetables in the market. Her braid went tossing back and forth until finally my father pulled her mouth to his. I wanted to run away like the wind, and at the same time I wanted to keep staring at them forever. A swarm of flies hung around the shaded lamp like a swatch of gauze. The poplar outside the depot looked like a real tree up to the eaves, but there the gutter cut off the light and it became a black tower, swaying and rustling. But the crickets were even louder, and nothing cut them off, from the grass all the way up to the sky, so that I could see Papa's open mouth but not hear him. I lost track of how long I had been watching or how long the sin lasted. I wanted to make it home on time, to beat him there by a decent interval. The shortest route led through a hole in the fence behind the main building.

Farther away from the depot, the buildings along the avenue seemed to dissolve in the light of the streetlamps. The thick, whitewashed tree trunks shimmered and reeled, or was it me not walking straight. After what I'd seen, I could no longer allow myself to be frightened of the night lurking among the trees. And besides, I knew that even during the day, when the sun was glaring, the white gravestones in the children's section of the cemetery would reel exactly the same way as the whitewashed tree trunks were doing in the moonlight. I knew that, because the boy I had made the dust snakes with was lying in the cemetery behind the bread factory. In the heat of the dog days, when children had to stay indoors, his stone looked as drunk as the avenue did at night. The markers around him tottered and swayed, especially the portraits on the gravestones, the ones showing children with soft toys and pacifiers. The boy with the largest gravestone was sitting astride a snowman.

Before I was born, my parents had had a boy who turned blue in a fit of laughing. He never became a real son, since he died before he was christened. My parents had no qualms about releasing his grave plot after just two years. It wasn't until one day when I was eight years old and a boy with grazed knees was sitting across from us in the tram that Mama whispered in my ear:

If your brother had lived, we wouldn't have had you.

The boy was sucking candy molded in the shape of a duck, it swam in and out of his mouth, outside I saw the houses rising through the windows as we passed. I was sitting next to Mama on a hot wooden seat that was painted green—sitting there in place of my brother.

We had two pictures of me from the maternity home, but not a single one of my brother. One picture shows me on a pillow, next to Mama's ear. In the other I'm in the middle of a table. With their second child my parents wanted one picture for themselves and one for the gravestone.

I was too old to be frightened of the whitewashed tree trunks on the way home from the depot. But I felt more degraded because of my father than I had in the tram because of Mama. I'm better than that girl with her braid, I thought, why doesn't Papa take me. She's dirty, her hands are green from all the vegetables. What does he want with her, she has a good husband. I see him in the mornings on my way to school. He's young, he lugs those heavy baskets for her from the bus stop to the market, while she just carries a plastic bag. Besides, she has a child, who patiently passes the time in the back of her stall, underneath the concrete roof, playing with a grubby stuffed dog on an upturned wooden crate. Fool that I am, I even bought an armful of horseradish from her the day before yesterday. She dropped the money into a large apron pocket over her belly and stroked the child's hair. She knew who I was, she must have been thinking about her sin. A fresh cold sore was blossoming on her upper lip, it never occurred to me that she had caught it from Papa. His own was fading, it had been a vivid crimson two weeks earlier. You couldn't tell by looking at her how happy she would have been to leave the child and his grubby plush dog at home in order to have some fun with my father come evening.

Papa showed up at home carrying my bag over his shoulder, he placed it in front of me and asked:

Since when have you been so careless.

Who's calling who careless, I asked back.

He pretended not to hear, sat down at the table under the bright light and waited for his food. He cut the salami into pieces thick as a finger and ate four red-hot peppers he'd brought with him, probably from her. It's possible he even paid for them. And to top it all off he ate six slices of bread and a handful of salt. That long braid must be a real drain on his energy. Maybe the gas fumes in the bus got his blood pumping to his heart too fast, and that made him feel spunky, like back during the war. My grandfather had once shown me a small picture and said:

That's his tank.

And who's that, I asked.

Lying in the grass next to my father was a young woman, barefoot, her shoes flung far apart at the base of a shrub. Dandelions were blooming between her calves, her elbow was bent and her head propped on her hand.

A musical girl, Grandfather said, she played his flute. During the war your father was after anything with a slit that didn't eat grass. Later the letters never stopped coming. I tore them all up so your mother wouldn't see them. I was amazed how quickly he married her. She wasn't so much to look at really, but she put a bridle on him, and had him where she wanted from the get-go.

I rode to the depot with him ten more evenings, counting each trip on my fingers. I grabbed his arm, his knee, but he just kept his eyes on the road. I touched his ear, he smiled at me, then looked back at the road. I placed my hand on his, on the wheel. He said:

I can't drive like this.

On the last trip I offered him a pear I'd already taken a large bite out of, so he wouldn't have to struggle with the thick, yellow peel. He chewed and smacked his lips, the juice frothing around his teeth, and swallowed with an absent look in his eyes. Papa liked the taste, but I was only eating to entice him.

When I couldn't stomach any more and he turned his mouth to take another bite, I said:

You can have the rest, I've had enough.

He could have asked why. He was honking as he turned the corners because he was looking forward to his woman with the long braid. He was sailing through the red lights, not to give us something to laugh about but because he was in a hurry to see her.

When he reached the depot on that last trip, he once again opened the bus door at the gates with a flourish that was part of his sin. He'd eaten the rest of the pear, including the core, and tossed the stalk through the door before I could get out. Now he was ready for forbidden flesh.

After that I stayed home in the evening. At least he might have asked whether I wanted to come along just one more time. I'd used up all ten fingers, but I could easily have started over. Maybe cigarettes would have worked better than my hands or a half-eaten pear. I could have taught him how to inhale the smoke into his lungs; Papa just puffed the smoke out through his mouth—in fact, he only smoked because the foreign cigarettes made him look smart. And since he couldn't afford them, he rarely smoked at all, but smoking somehow fit him. While he was taking the bus in for the night, I would pick a peach from the pitch-black trees along our fence and plop down on the garden bench. I'd listen to the crickets chirping a song about a bus that changed into a bed in the evenings, intimate and sinful and just for two. Actually for three, since that was the secret I was eating and swallowing.

When I came home from my last ride, after the pear had failed to get me anywhere, Mama asked:

Have you been crying.

73

Yes, I had been.

There was a dog prowling around the garbage cans, he followed me from the avenue all the way to the bread factory, I told her. Mama said:

It's in heat and you scared it.

All you think about is being in heat, I yelled: it's nothing but skin and bones and it's half-dazed with hunger.

My heart turned so hard, it would have struck her dead if I had thrown it. My tongue dried out, that was how much I hated her when she added, without a trace of shame:

Ah, so that's why I heard that howling outside.

Outside, as always in dry summers at dusk, there was not a single dog to be heard, nothing except the chirping of crickets, from the ground all the way up to the sky. Mama was simply dressing up my lie with my being scared of a dog in heat. She was lying to keep me from blurting out that it was my father who was in heat, and that I could have made him scared if I had wanted.

How often have I had to lie or keep my mouth shut to protect the people I love most—at the very times I could stand them least—to keep them from plunging headlong into some disaster. Whenever I wanted my hatred to last forever, a feeling of disgust would soften it up. With a hint of love on the one hand, and a heap of self-reproach on the other, I was already surrendering to the next hatred. I've always had just enough sense to spare others, but never enough to save myself from misfortune.

One evening my mother put on her summer dress with the tight rows of mother-of-pearl buttons and the daring low-cut back, did her hair up in a French twist, fastened it with a few barrettes, and popped a caramel into her mouth. Any time she sucked on sweets while doing herself up, she had something in

74

mind that required some finesse. She put on her white sandals and said:

What a hot day. Now it looks like it's cooled off a little. I think I'll go out for a stroll along the avenue.

I'm not sure whether she managed to slip through the gap in the fence wearing that tight dress. When she arrived at the depot, her husband was fixing his engine's cooling system. He must have kept a hold on himself, as Lilli would have said, when he saw the daring low-cut back, the hairstyle, and the white sandals. Perhaps he had her sit behind the wheel to wait until he'd finished making the repairs. They walked home arm in arm, the white sandals shimmering with the tree trunks. At supper she said:

Nobody's paying you to spend every evening doing repairs after a long day's work.

Are you kidding. I make more runs than anyone else, he said, that way I'll get the bonus after New Year's. Why else would I do it.

Mama raised her eyebrows, she even got up from her chair and cut the bread for herself and for him, although the loaf and knife were next to his plate. My grandfather and I had to cut it for ourselves.

After Papa died my mother set the table with one plate less, as if it were the most natural thing in the world. She did not lose her appetite and, to judge by appearances, she slept better. The rings under her eyes disappeared. She didn't grow any younger, but she did stand still as time passed. Apathy makes you neglect your appearance, but she wasn't like that. Her dishevelment was more on the inside: either she had found pride in her loneliness, or else she was so cut adrift that she was no longer herself. Neither happy nor sad—merely beyond all changes of facial expression. There was more life in a glass of water. When she dried herself she became like the towel, when she cleared the dishes she became like the table, and she became like the chair when she sat down. One year after Papa's death, Grandfather said:

You've got all the time in the world. You should go into town more often. Maybe you'll meet a man you like. Having someone younger than me around for the yardwork wouldn't be so bad, either.

Shouldn't you be keeping me from doing that, said Mama. After all, my husband was your son.

I'm not like that, though.

But you didn't remarry.

No, I didn't, but then again, your husband didn't die in the camp, Grandfather said.

It was all for nothing. Mama no longer did her hair up in a French twist, and she retired the tight dress with the daring low-cut back. She didn't want to put a bridle on anyone else. She no longer had any curiosity, not even about her child, who had flown the coop and rarely came home.

When my grandfather died, I stayed only one night at home with her. The next afternoon I went back to the city. She could have asked me to stay longer; after all, I'd taken two days' leave. My bed was covered with plastic bags full of her winter clothes; I slept on the couch, and she thought nothing of it. Before I had to leave to catch my train, she set the table. She laid out two plates and ate without noticing that I was only going through the motions. She used to tell me that I was just being finicky if I wasn't hungry. Now she no longer cared.

For all those years we had had four plates on the table. That seemed normal since there were four of us living in the house. Until Mama confessed that they'd only had me because my brother had died. From then on there were five of us, and one of us was eating off my brother's plate, although I didn't know which one. My brother had never had a chance to eat from it.

He had his mouth clamped on her nipple but had stopped drinking, my grandfather said. We didn't realize that he wasn't asleep, that he . . .

Because the fifth plate was never put on the table, the other four didn't stay there long, either. When Papa died, the first plate became redundant. My moving to the city cleared the second from the table. Grandfather's death meant the third was no longer needed.

The tram is listing to one side. Maybe the rails have buckled from the heat. The old lady has something wrong with her nerves, her head is shaking left and right, as if she were constantly saying no. Are we almost at the market, she asks. The driver says: Not for a while yet. The young man is standing by the rear door. We're only at the courthouse, he says, don't you come from around here. Of course I do, says the old woman, but yesterday I broke my glasses. I went to the optician's, but they didn't have a thing, no lenses, no glue, not a thing. Now I have to wait two whole weeks.

If only I were as old as she is, but it's impossible to swap places, not even with Lilli or Paul. I don't ever want to have to get off at the courthouse. It'll all come out at the trial, you'll speak there all right, says Albu whenever he doesn't like my answer. The driver pulls the third roll out of his shirt pocket, takes a bite and puts it down. He swallows and the mouthful goes tumbling down his throat. If we take too long I won't get any eggs today, says the old lady. The tram stops to let on a man in a suit carrying a briefcase. In that case I'll just buy plums, the old lady goes on, as she sizes up the new passenger, then giggles: The good thing about them is that they'll make it home in one piece. After all, plums don't break, you know. You can't bake a cake without eggs, says the driver, and a shot of rum and a lot of sugar. I know about you men, says the old lady, with your sweet tooth.

While Mama and I were eating after Grandfather's funeral, the broom keeled over in the corner of the room. The handle crashed against the floor. I had seen my father keel over, and it must have been the same with my grandfather. I picked up the glass of water. If Mama had been curious about how I was getting along, I would have told her about the lie in the factory, and about the death I had brought along with me in my new gray platform shoes. But the waterglass was unmoved. She stuffed a piece of bread crust into her mouth, then got up and stood the broom back in the corner.

Whenever a coat hanger dropped on the floor in the factory, or an umbrella fell in the tram, or a parked bicycle tipped over on the street, I could feel the cold vinyl, rushing in from both temples straight to the middle of my forehead. Mama was chewing and drinking a lot of water, she was more convinced than I was that she was my mother. She looked into her plate and said:

You know, once I started to send you a letter. I was sitting in the café, and it just occurred to me to write. It must have been May or July, and now, what month is it, that's right, it's already September. I went to the post office, put a stamp on the envelope, but then I forgot your address.

I looked into her eyes and let myself be taken in.

Do you still have it, I asked.

It's somewhere here on a piece of paper, I just have to find it.

I never called her Mother when I spoke to her, I just said You, the way you would to a child whose name you didn't know, anything more formal seemed inappropriate. Listening to her was tiresome, it didn't matter whether I said anything or not, just like it hadn't mattered when I left home for no real reason—I could just as well have stayed. After all, there were enough office jobs in our small town, even in the bread factory. As people say nowadays: that's just the way things turned out.

On my way to the station the air smelled of flour. The gate-keeper stood at the factory entrance, brushing dandruff off his uniform jacket. He doffed his cap and greeted me, I didn't recognize him. After I had passed, he yawned loudly. I spun around as if instead of the gatekeeper there had been a loose concrete slab gaping in the wake of my gray platforms and I was lucky to have escaped in the nick of time. Nothing was too far-fetched for that place, it could make evening come before the afternoon; it could pull the sun over and make it hang suspended in the sky behind the factory, glowing like a ball of fire, and then have it set inside the buildings, dark as a breadpan, before the day was done. I thought of the early evening hours after Papa's funeral. We came home from the cemetery, my grandfather went into the yard, turned on the faucet, and hauled the garden hose over to the peach trees. Mama called:

Not in your best suit, go and change.

I ran after him. Because of the drought, he said, as if the peaches would have died of thirst during the next quarter of an hour. The water squirted and gathered around the tree trunks in shallow pools, full of drowned ants. The earth drank slowly. Then Grandfather said:

You go out for a walk and the world opens up for you. And

before you've even stretched your legs properly, it closes shut. From here to there it's all just the farty sputter of a lantern. And they call that having lived. It's not worth the bother of putting on your shoes.

Now my grandfather had stretched his legs for the second time. I wanted to get on the train so as to ride through the cornfields before they turned black. Past the little railway stations that looked like doghouses. Be far away when Mama set the last plate on the table. Through all the years it must have been my brother's plate and my brother's hunger that kept her eating. That explains why she could cope so well alone, as if her table had never had more than a single plate.

When I looked at the light-blue train ticket, I knew how fortunate I'd been that my father hadn't tangled me up inside his love. His spunk was smarter than his brain. My good fortune that the promise of forbidden flesh meant more to him than the wetness of my half-eaten pear. Even in her wildest nightmares Mama didn't deserve to have me, in my youth, take her place and transport my father back to their first years of love, simply to secure our family against the woman with the long braid.

Things worked out differently for Lilli. Her mother's second husband was the first man Lilli could get her hands on.

He never became repulsive to me, Lilli said, but in time he did come to seem ordinary. The fact that we'd be at it as soon as my mother left the house became more of a habit than using the door handle.

Lilli's secret became history when she met the night porter with the war wound on the back of his neck. Until he retired, Lilli would join him after midnight and they would lie behind the wall of keys in the foyer. Later she spent her evenings in the storage room of a leather shop where the clothes were stacked up to the window, until the shopkeeper moved to the country with his wife. After that she made rounds at the hospital, until her night-duty doctor went to visit his brother-in-law in Buenos Aires and never came back. Later Lilli moved her love up to the afternoon and into the darkroom of a photographer she'd fallen for.

Having to hurry turns me on, said Lilli.

Sinning with her stepfather was ancient history, but Lilli's eyes still sharpened like cut glass when she said:

My mother sleeps with her second husband but tucks herself in with the death of her first.

Keeping a secret and having to hurry were more important to Lilli than feelings. Except for the old officer, every man with whom she began something had a wife at home. The first year, with her stepfather, was the riskiest and most beautiful. Later Lilli admitted that there was nothing so great about things being secret. That's just how it always turned out. The real secret is why love starts out with claws like a cat and then fades with time like a half-eaten mouse, she said.

Lilli was German. Just after he married, her father was drafted and then blown to pieces by a mine during the war. Lilli's mother was two months pregnant. As a war widow she received two care packages every year from the German Red Cross, one of them contained the quilt she had used ever since to cover herself up in bed. Another one had the blue skirt with the accordion pleats that Lilli wore, because it was too tight for her mother. Even if nobody else had a skirt like that, it was still far from pretty. It was made of some hard thin material that glistened as if it had just been drenched in water. You expected it to start dripping around the hem. I said:

It might work for old women, a little corrugated tin around the hips to hide the widows' flab.

So what, it's practical, and the blue matches my eyes, said

Lilli. Whenever she talked about her mother, she would also mention the dead soldier who never had the chance to be her father. Occasionally we'd be in the city, she'd take out her wallet, and I could see the white scalloped edge of a photo sticking out. Once I asked her:

⌐ Who's that you've got inside there.

Lilli stashed the wallet back in her coat, then said:

My father.

Is he a secret, I asked.

Yes.

Why talk about him, then.

Because you came right out and asked.

First you talked about him and then I asked.

I never said a thing about the picture.

Well you might as well go on and show it to me, if he's right there.

How can he be right here if he's dead, she said.

I fanned my forehead with my hand:

⌐ Are you nuts.

Lilli took the picture out of the wallet and held it out for me to see. He wasn't even twenty, he had a wry smile and was wearing a jagged white daisy in the buttonhole of his tunic. Lilli had the same nose and eyes. I reached for the picture, Lilli shoved my hand away:

You can look but you can't touch.

I tapped on Lilli's forehead with my index finger.

You're cuckoo.

Seen enough.

No, you keep shaking it.

Then Lilli turned the photo upside down, so her father seemed to be hanging by his legs. Upside down or not I immediately noticed that the collar insignia and the front of his cap had been inked over—those places were glossy, although the picture itself was matte. Embarrassment usually makes people's eyes go narrow, but hers were wide open and forgot how to blink. Lilli was spoiling for an argument, but not because of the inked-out spots on the uniform.

Put it away, I said.

Why, you're slurping him up with your eyes.

I'm sorry, I shouted.

What does that mean, you're sorry, she asked.

Are you jealous.

Maybe you are, he's much too young for me.

Right now he'd be just right.

I never thought of that.

But I did, I said.

Every day after work I was happy to be rid of Nelu. I paced up and down the tram stop in front of the low, grimy buildings, the windows of which protruded slightly over the pavement. Behind the curtains, lights were already burning in the winter afternoon. Patches of ice gleamed in the potholes like spilt milk, trucks were rumbling past, whirling up the snow behind them, and in the whirls, I saw the boy with his dust snakes. He could run better ever since he was dead, and my father could drive better too. But the street swallowed the rumbling and the whirls of snowy dust and then forgot where it was going. I let one tram go by, then two, three. Paul worked an hour and a half longer than I did, anyway. There was nothing to go home to. Other trucks drove by, if I was in luck there'd be a bus among them as well.

Last summer after work Paul again had to ride his motorbike home barefoot, shirtless, and wearing borrowed trousers.

While he was in the shower everything he'd been wearing had disappeared—shirt, trousers, underpants, socks, and sandals. Although a guard had been posted in the changing room ever since spring, it was the fourth time that summer that Paul had finished his shower and found he had nothing more than his bare skin. Stealing isn't considered such a bad thing in the factory. The factory belongs to the people, you belong to the people, and whatever you take is collectively owned, anyway—iron, tin, wood, screws, and wire, whatever you can get your hands on. They like to say:

By day you take, by night you steal.

So one man loses his socks, another his shirt, a third his shoes. Even before the guard was there, nobody was robbed as often as Paul. And he was the only one who had everything taken all at once. His clothes were hardly worth the taking. The thief was more concerned with embarrassing Paul by leaving him stark naked in the factory than with taking his things. Someone was out to humiliate him. Paul looked carefully at the other men as they talked, laughed, ate, he studied how they worked, watched them shuffle up and down the hall. Now they're all going about their usual business, thought Paul, but there'll come a time when whoever is doing this will forget himself and make a mistake. Then Paul would settle accounts in front of everybody.

How do you mean, I asked.

I'll beat him until he squeaks like a mouse.

Some people cry out when you beat them, so it's clear when they've had enough. But others just go silent, and then you go on hitting them till they're dead. I was afraid that Paul was working himself up to a state of blindness, and I said:

The thing to do with someone who steals clothes is strip

84

him naked and run him through the factory, then he'll be even smaller than a mouse, and you won't be guilty of anything.

It could be anybody. If it turns out to be one of the old fellows, or some rickety kid with ears bigger than his feet, I'll take him outside for a little chat.

There are enough clothes around, just think if someone had stolen your precious skin, Paul's workmates said. I heard your nipples caught cold yesterday. All soaped up and waiting and not a masseuse in sight.

Paul laughed along with the others. He preferred the few jokers to the silent herd with their sluggish tongues and dead eyes. But the difference between them was of no help to Paul in finding out the thief. Either the man made no mistakes, or else Paul didn't notice them. Even Paul's set of spare clothes, which, like everybody else, he kept in a tool cabinet just for this possibility, had disappeared after the shower.

Socialism sends its workers forth into the world unclad, Paul said in the factory. Every week or so it's as if you were born anew. It keeps you young.

When the jokers showed up in the morning, they greeted him with:

Naked morning.

When they were eating they said:

Enjoy your naked meal.

Before they left for home:

Have a naked evening.

At the Party meeting the distinction between jokers and sheep no longer applied, said Paul. There, everybody sat in the second to last row, just like a wooden fence. The sweat was dripping off their temples, their hair was stuck to their skulls, and you couldn't tell whether it was from the sun or fear. In order to avoid appearing as if they wanted to speak, they never moved their hands from their laps, just kept them there, dirty, hard, and motionless against their knees. The curtains at the front of the assembly hall were drawn shut, so that the presidium and the first rows of chairs were in shadow, but these seats were empty, except for Paul. He had to stand there and deliver public self-criticism for his quip, then sit down by himself in one of the shadowy rows on a seat that creaked even when you breathed. And he had to breathe in deeply, because even the air seemed to shrink back before him.

Paul said that when he joined the Party he was still a kid, a tenth-grader from the mechanical engineering school. Paul's mother said:

In this country you can be as smart as a whip but without a red book all you can do is stand on your beak and fart in the dust like a partridge.

She was a village girl who'd left her turnips for a life in the city. She moved into heavy industry, where there were five times as many men as women. With the lower half of her body she joined the Party, learning the ABC's of communism lying on her back in various beds.

Molded and crowned, said Paul. Well, what choice did she have, all she knew how to do was hoe, sew, reap, backstitch a little with the sewing machine, dance, and milk ewes. Her political praxis stopped at the foot of the bed, yet she understood exactly at what age a well-endowed girl should stop changing men. She never lost that instinct, and when she was a hairsbreadth away from losing more than she stood to gain, she married Paul's father, a Hero of Socialist Labor. She became faithful, and faithful she remained. Her husband wanted to teach her the language of the Party. Her brain was intelligent, but her tongue was much too loose for a language devoid of smell and taste, hearing and sight. No matter what Paul's father recited to her, the words in her mouth sounded like a parody: In our strength lies progress.

Not so loud, he said.

Then it sounded feeble.

A little louder and it sounded affected.

You're talking about the cause, he said. You have to keep yourself out of it.

How's that, she asked, aren't I also part of our strength.

You can talk like that when you're bringing the sheep down from the mountain into the valley. At Party meetings just keep your trap shut.

The training lasted an entire January. Paul's mother said she'd rather clear all the snow off the mountain than talk this jargon. Her husband gave up.

Although Paul hadn't said a word to anybody, after only three days people in the factory knew I'd moved into his place in the leaning tower. His mother found out just as quickly. She sent her son a letter that was written in a shaky hand and riddled with mistakes. It began:

Light of my life, my own flesh and blood.

It went on: There are girls who are like flowers or angels. But you, my son, are wrapping yourself in a rag that everyone's already used to wipe themselves. This woman loves neither you nor her country. She will poison your heart. Do not let her cross my threshold. You are throwing your life into the dirt. I beg you, my child, finish with her.

She hadn't written *Your mother* beneath the kisses but her own signature, practiced and ornate, as if she were a more refined, more cultured lady. Paul was convinced that someone had dictated the letter. The terms of endearment she normally used were as familiar to him as her handwriting.

87

And what about that signature.

Oh, that's hers, said Paul.

His father had taught her how to sign things, and it came as easily to her as darning socks or milking ewes. Paul's father believed the signature reflected the man, that people can learn more from your signature than from your eyes. His wife rarely had to write, but she often had to sign forms in the factory, so after that unsuccessful January he at least taught her how to sign things with a flourish, using newspaper edges for practice. That letter is why to this day I've never met Paul's mother. A year after his father died, when she stopped wearing black, she sent Paul a letter with her picture. It shows a woman with permed hair, and a round face a little bloated with age, giving a kindly impression. A retired machine fitter, sitting in a café for the first time after her year of mourning, eating cake. Short sleeves, baggy skin around the elbows. On her wrist she's wearing a man's watch, and holding a small spoon using all five fingers. Her left hand is pressing her handbag tight in her lap.

Paul tells the story of how at one meeting she didn't keep her trap shut and raised her hand to complain about a draft in the hall.

Men have it good, she said, they put on two pairs of long trousers and don't catch cold, but you know that wind blows right up our coozies. Everybody laughed, but she just looked at them wide-eyed and then corrected herself:

As I was saying, that wind blows right up our private affairs.

On the way home after the meeting, Paul's father hit her, saying:

Don't you understand that you're making a fool of me as well.

He gave vent to his rage on the street, he couldn't put it off.

Maybe this was because he knew that by the time they got home he would no longer have the nerve to hit her, and after that he never hit her again. From then on she was nicknamed Private Affairs, and inside the factory the name stuck until the day she retired.

Before Paul and I got married, the chief engineer called him in and said:

You've really landed one there. That lady thinks you're one of her Marcellos. You've still got time to pull out.

I couldn't have cared less what the man said. But Paul overdid it with his answer, which, like most appropriate responses, was too risky:

I wanted to marry Stalin's daughter, but unfortunately she's already spoken for.

Our wedding came close on the heels of that answer, with the chief engineer waiting for Paul to make his next false move. If Paul hadn't talked about socialism sending its workers forth into the world unclad, some other pretext would have been discovered. False steps can always be found, unlike stolen clothes.

Thank God the tram doesn't stop on the bridge. I don't want to have to look at the river, I don't like what it carries. Whether it's reflecting what it has seen or whether it's washing those same sights away in rippling waves, it turns everyone's heads, in fact it sticks in my throat. But I can't help looking. The willows seem larger than usual, the river is low in the hot weather. The sun is passing above it, flickering with hot, needle-like rays. The man with the briefcase is slouched on his seat, squinting in the glare. It occurs to him that his briefcase could work as a sunshade and he places it against the window. That helps me as well: if the river hadn't addled my brain I could keep my eyes fixed on the briefcase, which looks like a secret door in the middle of the car. There are papers stowed inside the briefcase, probably court papers, with names, official stamps, signatures, and a criminal charge. Whenever the court is involved it's a bad omen. Is this man a lawyer trying to go over everything one last time in peace and quiet, or is he one of the accused, released on his own recognizance shortly before his final hearing. Either way, he's in pretty good shape—at least he knows what's in his file. Besides, it's not even nine and he's already on his way to work, while I've been summoned for ten sharp. He's dressed neatly. Can a defendant who is preparing for court early in the morning still pay attention to matching cuff links, trouser creases, polished shoes, and a close shave. Obviously he'd have plenty of reason to do so; unlike the judge, he has to make the perfect impression, even if it doesn't have any real bearing on the case. Or is the man with the briefcase simply vain, maybe he always looks like he's just been unwrapped, no matter where he's going or what the time of day—but that requires a job that doesn't involve getting dirty. Of course he could be both judge and defendant—surely cases like that aren't unheard of. Serious mistakes often have silly explanations; no doubt even men with matching cuff links get charged with crimes. Including judges who know the law by heart. But what if their children do something that's not permitted. They, too, grow up and move away from home and aren't any different from Lilli and me. Who is my mother, anyway: nobody paid the slightest bit of attention to her when I wrote the notes. Papa was dead, Lilli's stepfather had already retired. If he or my father had been judges, what kind of questions might Lilli have asked before attempting to flee, what would I have asked before writing my notes. Even judges' children hear something about the world, they go to the Black Sea like everyone else in this country. They look out and feel the same urge to go somewhere, feel it tugging at them from head to toe. You don't have to be particularly bad off to think: This can't be all the life I get. The judges' children know as well as Lilli and me that the same sky that looks down on the border guards stretches all the way to Italy or Canada, where things are better than here. They demand their good luck, although not of the border guards. One person pleads with God, the other with the empty sky. No matter whom they appeal to, sometimes it ends well, and sometimes it ends red as a bed of poppies, or in being left behind, alone, like Lilli's officer, or else all over the place like me. One way or the other, the attempt will be made, whether sooner or later, in this way or that.

Paul came home barefoot since the shoes his workmates had lent him didn't fit. This time he didn't need a shirt, it was a hot summer. But he did borrow a pair of trousers that stopped a few inches above his ankles and were three times too big around, he'd tied some wire through the waistband. At home Paul made fun of his appearance and pranced about the hall. The seat of his trousers billowed down to the back of his knees. He stretched his arms out and whirled me around, faster and faster. I put my ear to his mouth, he hummed a song, closed his eyes, and pressed my hand against his chest. I could feel the swift pounding through my hand and said:

Don't charge around like this, your heart is fluttering like a wild dove.

We danced more slowly, keeping our elbows in front of us and sticking our behinds out so our stomachs and legs had room to swing. Paul bumped me on the left hip, spun around, bumped me on the right, and then his stomach danced away from me, and my hips swung up and down of their own accord. My head was empty except for the beat.

This is how old people dance, he said. You know, when my mother was young, she had pointy hips. My father called them tango bones.

I stepped on Paul's dusty toes with my own red-tipped ones and sang:

World world sister world
when shall I tire of you.
When my bread is dry
when my hand forgets my glass
when the coffin's boxed me in
maybe that's when I'll be tired of you.
Living is despairing
and the dead they rot away . . .

We felt so together, we laughed our way through the song, in which death seems like a special prize following a life that's been paid for dearly. We gulped down the song as we laughed and never once missed a beat. Suddenly Paul pushed me away and yelled:

Ow, the zipper's pinching me.

I tried to open it but couldn't. He pulled the wire out of the belt loops and tossed it in the corner, the seat dropped to his heels, but some pubic hair was snagged in the zipper. I was supposed to cut the hairs that had got caught, but I was laughing too hard. Paul took the scissors away from me, his hands shaking:

Just get out of the way, would you.

Where to, I asked.

So I let Paul do it himself, but I couldn't stop laughing,

gurgling more and more, as if I were having a fit. I laughed and laughed until I finally got over it. I inhaled deeply and immediately exhaled, the air was exploding inside me until I had no more, and that was the end. But the beginning was happiness itself. To dance to the rhythm of laughter. And to snap the short leash that otherwise kept us tied. It had to have been happiness if a song about death could warm our temples from within. Until we felt ashamed in front of each other, until the leash shrank to a length shorter than our noses: that's how long our happiness lasted. Then Paul ran his hand through his hair, and I curled up my fingers and dug my nails into my palms like a scolded child.

The silence after our happiness felt as if the furniture had broken out in goose bumps. We fell flat on our faces, right back into our hopelessness, especially Paul. He was always afraid we might grow used to happiness. While I kept laughing, he had cut the snagged hairs, the scissors were again hanging on the wall, beside the keys, the huge borrowed trousers lay in the corner. Still in just his underpants, Paul stepped from the room into the hall and stood in the sunlight, in a long rectangular patch that crossed the floor and part of the wall. The sunlight sliced through the shadow cast by his legs right above the knees.

Why do you always go on laughing until you gloat, he asked.

That sounded like Nelu saying:

There you go again, happy in your own filthy, ass-backward way.

Nelu had something there, I was happy because I needed to be. When it came to hurting people, Nelu was the expert. But my tongue was quicker than his, and my hands were more adroit. He would miss whiskers on his chin while shaving, and when he made coffee the heating element would fall out of the mug. When it came to tying his shoelaces he was all thumbs, it took forever, and they were never properly tied. He had a great deal to say on the subject of buttons, but he was incapable of sewing one on.

Bungled again, I'd say to him, when he messed something up.

Every few days he'd bang his head against the cabinet door. Or else he'd drop his freshly sharpened pencil, bend to pick it up, and forget that the drawer above his head was still open. He'd have a fresh bruise, and I would say:

Another violet coming into bloom.

And laugh until he left me with my contempt and skipped out to the factory yard, where he still counted as somebody in the eyes of others. No matter how long he stayed away, I'd still be laughing when he came back, or else I'd start up again. He would massage his fresh bruise, next to the greenish-blue ones from before.

It's possible that my laughing fits over Nelu were similar to those with Paul. But the contempt I felt for Nelu was important, my laughter was sheer schadenfreude. As far as I was concerned, Nelu deserved whatever happened to him. And whatever happened was nowhere near enough. Fine with me if Nelu couldn't stand my ass-backward happiness. But mine wasn't filthy—his was. He maneuvered me into a corner until I wound up getting the sack. Because being able to shave smoothly or tie your shoelaces or sew on a button doesn't mean much in the factory. The abilities that count there are completely different . . .

Of course I enjoyed my ass-backward happiness all the more after Nelu had done his worst. After the first notes, my laughter sounded as though I couldn't care less about his denunciation. Even so, I was powerless to ward off the harm he inflicted.

When we had finished dancing, Paul drove into town on his Java to buy two pairs of shoes: one to put on now and a spare to stash in the tool cabinet. I watched him take off, the red Java down on the street looked as beautiful as the red enamel coffee tin on the kitchen table. I stepped through the patch of sunlight in the hall, at a loss for what to do with myself. Inside the storage closet I came across my first pair of wedding shoes, they were white. My second pair were brown. They were lying underneath Paul's sandals with the worn-out soles, the ones from last summer. Autumn had come overnight, a low sky, rain pressing the rotting leaves down into the earth. And overnight we stopped wearing our summer things and needed what money we had for buying winter clothes rather than spending it on expensive new half-soles for the sandals. The weather alone was reason enough not to take summer sandals to the shoemaker's. They'd have to wait a while before it was their turn. We could scarcely manage the barest necessities.

The patch of sunlight was now entirely on the floor, but it still refused to touch the borrowed trousers. I didn't touch them, either. The silence in our apartment was the kind that makes you feel you're filling the whole space, from the floor all the way to the ceiling, which isn't possible. Even a plate falling off the table or a picture falling off the wall—as if my father were dying all over again—would have been better. I crossed the patch of sunlight into the room and with wary hands I shut the window, although not without first looking out: there on the sidewalk, where no ordinary person is allowed to park, two people were sitting in a red car. One was gesticulating, the other was smoking. I walked out of the room into the hall, into the kitchen, back into the hall. I know what it's like when you're pacing back and forth, unable to remember what it was you had just set out to do—until it finally occurs to you. Back and forth on the floor, shuffling or stepping too deliberately, just getting away from wherever you happen to be. I tossed the wedding shoes into the storage closet and closed the door. But I kept Paul's sandals and wiped off the cobwebs. A squashed blackberry was stuck to the right sole. Either that or the red car suddenly brought everything back: last summer at the river, Paul naked after showering at the factory, dancing together in the hall, the rough way Paul had grabbed the scissors from my hand.

Instead of these thoughts we're constantly mulling over, it would be better to have the actual things inside your head, so you could reach in and touch them. People you want, or people you want to be rid of. Objects you've held on to or lost. There would be an order to things in my head: in the center would be Paul, but not my clutching at him and running away from him and loving him all at the same time. The sidewalks would run along my temples, as far as they like, and under my cheeks might be the shops with their glass display cases, though not my pointless destinations in the city. Of course there's no escaping Albu's lackey, who's probably sitting out there in the red car, waiting to ring our doorbell and give me my summons—not deliver, it's never in writing, so that I'm always left to worry whether Paul or I might have misheard the date. Albu's lackey would be lurking somewhere in the back of my head—and I'd prefer to have him there in person instead of his soft voice that eats right into me and is still stuck somewhere inside from the last time, and which pops right up the minute he's back at my door. The bridge over the river and my first husband with his suitcase would be in the back of my head, but not my suggestion that he go ahead and jump. And in my cerebellum, where we supposedly keep our sense of balance, would be a fly resting on a table, instead of an evening meal chewed and swallowed with no appetite. Surfaces and contours would be divided into friends and foes, easy to tell apart. And in between there'd still be some space for happiness.

I took some newspaper and wrapped up the sandals, but then changed my mind and put them in a plastic bag, since I didn't want to walk past the red car carrying a bundle of papers. I wanted to do something special for Paul, because I had laughed too long. And I wanted to know what the two faces in the car looked like. In the end I couldn't say whether it was the faces or Paul's sandals that drew me out into the street.

There are people who distinguish not only between objects and thoughts, but also between thoughts and feelings. I wonder how. It's inconceivable that the swallows strung out among the clouds above the beanfield should have exactly the same wingtips as Nelu's mustache, but that's only a misperception. As with all misperceptions, I can't tell whether it's the objects themselves or the thoughts about them that account for the error. But since that's the way it is, the mind has to share in the burden and take on as many misperceptions as the earth has trees. I folded two fifty-leu notes into small squares, and picked them up in one hand along with the plastic bag. The elevator door opened, my face bounced into the mirror before I followed with my feet. The floor clanked as the elevator started down.

I walked right up to the red car, I wanted both of them to see that the world is full of misperceptions and that I could come down to them instead of their coming up. Through the open window of the car I asked:

Have you got a light.

I wanted to add: That's okay, I don't really smoke, I just wanted to know if you had a light. I had imagined they would both give me a light right away, in order to get rid of me, but I was wrong. Everything turned out differently. The man shook his head, and the woman snapped at me:

Can't you see we're not smoking.

He pounded the steering wheel and laughed as if she'd scored a big hit. The letters *A* and *N* flashed on his signet ring, and the woman's hair gleamed crow-black in the sun while she whispered something in his ear. Her face was an oily tan from sunbathing, and around her neck hung a speckled seashell necklace. I said:

You could have been smoking before, and you might light up again after I'm gone. Or perhaps I should say you might go on necking.

Hey, miss, she said, in case you haven't gotten fucked today because your husband's banging whores after work, why don't you go to the bar and get yourself one of those guys with a big cock. He'll knock those fancy ideas out of you.

You must be joking, I said, I'd rather wait until my man comes home, he's got a cock the size of a telephone pole that hoists me right up to heaven.

Of course they hadn't been necking: they did that someplace else. She turned spiteful so fast she must have felt as if I'd caught her in the act. And he must have felt the same way, or else he wouldn't have sat there small and dumb as a turd. He was probably on duty, and she was helping him pass the time. Before she rolled up the window, I said:

From what I hear, the ones who aren't getting any are all wearing seashell necklaces this summer, or is that just dried pigeon shit.

Her seashell necklace really did look exactly like that. Walking away, I could hear my own footsteps; I felt a little nauseous. The door to the bar was open, instead of looking inside I looked at the linden trees, which I knew weren't drunk. But I couldn't help hearing the drunken voices. The smell of brandy, coffee, smoke, disinfectant, and the dust of summer followed close behind me.

For the first time there was no music playing at the shoemaker's. The cassette recorder with the batteries held in place by a piece of elastic was not in its usual place on the table. A young man sat behind the workbench, his teeth protruding so that his lips never fully closed over his mouth. Since he wasn't wearing an apron I supposed he was the shoemaker's son-in-law, the accordion player. I asked after the old shoemaker. The young man crossed himself four times and said:

Dead.

Where is he buried, I asked.

He fished about in a drawer, I assumed for a piece of paper, but he pulled out a cigarette.

Are you here to look for graves or to have your shoes fixed.

I unwrapped the shoes from the newspaper, he blew the smoke straight out and watched my fingers, as if the shoes might explode at any moment.

Had he been sick, I asked.

He nodded.

What did he have.

No money, said the young man.

Did he kill himself.

How do you get that.

I don't know, I'm asking you.

He shook his head.

A young man can't be blamed for an old man's dying, I thought, but he could at least have some sympathy. All that matters to this wry-face is that a place became available in a row of shops where customers pass by from morning till night.

He stubbed out the cigarette in a tin can and said:

The grave's on Mulberry Street, is that good enough, or am I supposed to know which row it's in.

That's good enough for more than you think.

My feelings exactly, he said. Ever since I came here in March I've had to talk about the old shoemaker.

I thought you were his son-in-law, I said.

God forbid. My first day here this guy shows up with so many black and yellow bruises he looked like a canary, and starts clearing out the workshop right under my nose. All the leather, hammers, pegs and lasts, buckles and nails, he took the whole works, even the emery paper and polishes and brushes. These things don't come with the workshop, he told me. What do you mean, I said: I didn't bring anything with me, I left everything to the person who took over my place in Josefstadt district. He said he could sell the stuff to me if I wanted. You know, at home they were waiting for me to start earning something, they didn't have enough money in the house to buy a loaf of bread. But I'm not so crazy as to pay for what's already mine.

The old man had a lot of customers, I said, that means he must have had some money, too.

His daughter drank her way through the money, the young man said, and she beat up on the son-in-law, which is why he looked the way he did. When he was clearing out the place, I asked him if he was also a shoemaker. He spread out his pitiful white fingers and said: Are you kidding, do I look like you. So I asked the man what he wanted the stuff for. To play the accordion, he said. Oh, I said, so that's how you got the bruises. No, he said, my wife gave me those. I wondered whether I should go to the bar and get the two policemen who are always sitting there. But the locals still don't know me, so that would have only caused trouble. The accordion player might have said it was me who had turned him into a canary. On second thought I really should have given him another black eye, he deserved it.

The only trees on Mulberry Street are acacias. There's an alcoholic who lives at one end of the street. At the other end lies Lilli. And now the shoemaker as well. The old man was short and skinny, but he had big hands and rounded fingernails that the leather had discolored a beautiful brown so they looked like ten roasted pumpkin seeds. Whenever I went to his shop he would run his hand over his head as if he still had his hair. The sweat would bead up on his bald spot while the cassette recorder played folk music at low volume, and his head shone like the glass balls people place in the flower beds around their houses. It looked like it might shatter the instant he banged into something.

So, you've danced those shoes to pieces again, he joked. Actually I don't know if he was joking. All I know is that just before I went and met the new shoemaker, I had danced, really for the first time in my life, to a song in which death comes like a special prize following a life that's been paid for dearly. After that evening in the restaurant I had never again danced with my first husband, and before that song I had never danced with Paul. I shouldn't have gone to the shoemaker's after dancing with Paul, I should have at least waited one more day, then the old man would still have been alive. It was my fault that he was dead.

Until his wife wound up in the asylum, the shoemaker had been a musician like his brother, brother-in-law, and son-in-law, who still play every evening in the restaurant on the Korso. Real musicians, he once said to me, they play from the soul—not from notes.

I don't like to dance and never wanted to be with another

man who did. The first thing I did when I met Paul was to bring up the question of dancing.

Paul said: Is it that important, I don't like dancing, women like dancing more than men. All the men I know feel they have to dance, said Paul. They dance with a woman half the night in order to fuck her afterwards for fifteen minutes.

What do you mean, my first husband likes dancing, I said, he loves it. You say it doesn't matter much, but you've never been married. Anytime there was music playing my husband became impossible to understand. He was addicted to dancing and I hated it and that tore us apart, and not just a little. Whenever there was music we were worlds apart. I turned into myself, became distant and dull, whereas he came out of himself and was in high spirits like a frisky monkey. We would argue, but we would have been better off if we'd kept silent, so that the rift would have remained small. But then when we were silent we would have been better off saying something, no matter how rude, since it's easier to get over a quarrel you've just had than the injuries you start listing in silence. The scene in the restaurant must have been near the beginning of September; we'd both taken our vacation. We didn't have enough money to go to the Black Sea or the Carpathians. So we were going to treat ourselves to a night on the town, and on the weekend we went out to a restaurant. My husband wanted to go to the Palace, on the Korso, where the shoemaker's family played the best music in the city. I thought it was too expensive. So that left the Central, where you can eat and dance for two hundred lei. Other people must have been watching their money as well, since the place was packed. The meat tasted a little sour, the coleslaw smelt like the powder you put out for flea beetles. Because white wine is pretty transparent it's easy to water down, so that was all they had. Most people were enjoying the food, using the bread to wipe their plates clean. They were chewing away like rabbits so they could get onto the dance floor as quickly as possible. And there I was, grumbling and dragging the dinner out. My husband ate faster than I did, although he was actually lingering over his dinner compared to the others. The orchestra was pretty lame but that was fine with me since I didn't want to dance. And it was fine with my husband because any music was good enough for him. I looked at the dance floor and saw that the people there felt the same way he did. Because they were all keeping an eye on their money, they had to make sure the evening was worth it, so they were all cheering. The men were crowing, the women were purring one moment and then yoo-hooing the next. At the end of a set they all looked up wide-eyed and laughed and their movements slowed until they were rocking back and forth like huge birds coming in to land. My husband had finished his meal and wiped his mouth with the napkin. His nose was bobbing inside his wineglass and looked warped. Above the table he remained stiff, but beneath the table his feet were tapping so that the floor was shaking. I said:

Maybe we're on a trip after all, the floor is shaking just like in a dining car. You people could dance to anything—a squeaky door or crickets chirping or whatever. Actually I shouldn't have said *you people,* including him with everyone else, seeing that he had to content himself with looking on and was suffering. He shoved his wineglass to the middle of the table, looked at me with long, narrow eyes, fixed so hard the corners looked like keyholes. He pursed his lips, whistled, and beat out the rhythm on the table with both hands. I said:

Now it's worse than a dining car, you must be going through withdrawal.

In a moment he'd need me to dance. In fact, he needed me now. The way he unpursed his lips, smiled briefly, and then went right on whistling. This compulsion to be so dashingly polite. His restraint, his avoiding any argument, just so I'll do what I'm told. The waiter cleared the table. Only our two glasses remained, trembling and transparent, as if they weren't really there, while we sat behind them, tingling with anticipation—I was spoiling for a fight, he was waiting for a dance. Eventually he won because he kept control of himself and because he let pass all the moments that could have led to an argument, in the end the whole thing seemed too stupid to me, anyway. Why had we spent all that money—we'd be missing it the very next day. He might as well get some compensation for the awful meal. I took his hand and led him onto the dance floor. We danced a path for ourselves through the couples, until we were right up next to the orchestra. He spun me around, the keys of the accordion blurred together like a Venetian blind.

You're dragging, my arm is falling asleep, he said.

I can't weigh less than I do.

Even the fattest women are light when they dance. But you're not dancing, you're just letting yourself droop.

He pointed out the fattest dancer in the restaurant, a matronly woman whom I had already noticed when we were eating. While she was at the table, I couldn't see much of her white dress with the black chess pieces, only that she pushed her plate practically to the middle of the table in order to be able to see it past her breasts. At the ends of her short, fat arms, her knife and fork barely reached the food.

That dress is billowing because it has deep pleats down the sides, not because she's so light on her feet. After all, I do know a thing or two about clothes, I said.

But not about women, he said.

The chess pieces came flying away from the white pleats. Snow and thistledown, my father-in-law's white horse, the wedding cake, the icing that scratched the tip of my nose. My head felt heavy. Even if I had to dance, I had no right to reproach my husband with his father, the Perfumed Commissar. I pulled myself together, but I did what I had not intended not to do. It's easy to tell other people not to do certain things, especially your nearest and dearest, but it's harder to tell yourself. As we danced past the swimming accordion keys, my brain went on tormenting me with scenes from the past, while my husband was enjoying being so near to the matronly woman. He touched the arm of the man who was leading the chess pieces and crowing out loud: Your partner dances well.

You bet she does. And I lead well, he said.

Then the matronly woman's dancing partner crowed once more, the matronly woman purred, and my husband crowed along with them.

If you crow like that once more, I said, I'm going to take off and run as far away as I can.

He crowed once again, but I kept my feet on the floor, and the matronly woman purred, and I didn't budge.

People were constantly switching partners. They paired off without a word being spoken. They were either following some intimate law between man and woman or else leaving it all up to chance. No requests were made and no consents were given. I lost the rhythm.

You're nothing more than a wisp but your bones turn to lead whenever you dance, said my husband.

Why don't you grab that tank, I said, then you'll have something to hold on to.

The old woman with the doddering head nudges me with her finger: Tell me, maybe you have an aspirin. No. But the driver has water, doesn't he, or maybe I didn't see right—no, he has a bottle. He has a bottle, I say. Her eyes had once been larger. As is often the case with old people, hers are webbed over with a very thin membrane like raw egg white growing in from the sides. Her two oval earrings, set with green stones, tremble along with her head. The constant shaking has stretched the holes in her earlobes into long slits that have practically been torn open. Toothpaste and a toothbrush are about all I could give her. The driver might have some aspirin, I say. The man with the briefcase reaches into his pocket: I think I have one left. A shriveled strip of cellophane crackles as he smoothes it flat: No—they're all gone, now I remember, I took the last one this morning. There's a pharmacy at the market, says the young man by the door. The old woman turns her head, I need the tablet now, not when we get to the marketplace. She moves up the tram from one row of seats to the next, steadying herself with both hands, until she reaches the middle of the car. The driver sees her in his mirror: Sit down, Grandma, you'll cause an accident. You should have taken the tram going the other way, it would have been quicker. The old woman totters up to him. What do you mean, I asked you and you said this was the right way. Do you at least have an aspirin.

If you're not in love, then dancing is worse than the crowd of people in the tram, I had said to my father-in-law. And if you are in love, then you have something better to do, a different way of stretching your legs, which can make you just as dizzy.

What do you mean, something better to do, he said, dancing isn't work, it's pleasure, if not an innate gift, a predisposition. And it's part of your culture. In the Carpathians they have different dances than they do in the hill country, and the ones by the sea are different from those along the Danube, and in the city they dance differently than they do in the country. You're supposed to learn to dance as a child. Your parents and family are supposed to teach you. Yours must have neglected their duty, and if you didn't learn you've really missed out.

No, I said, with my family it was more melancholy than neglect, after the camp nobody in our house had much zest for things like that.

A lot of water has flowed under the bridge since then, that was before you were born, he said. Some people's lives just don't work out and they're always coming up with excuses. Once upon a time they had some bad luck, and they blame everything on that. Come on, you might be too young to realize it, but I'm not. Believe me, even without the camp, life wouldn't have worked out for them.

It was New Year's Eve. The paraputch, as my father-in-law called the extended family, was celebrating in my in-laws' living room. I'll never know exactly what paraputch means. For me it sounded like a gang, because the family was so large and each member was shady in his own way. And although they couldn't stand one another, they were forever getting together. My father-in-law himself was at least two different people. He had the habit of making a nest for himself inside a person's breast, so as to be better able to kick him in the ribs later on.

David, Olga, Valentin, Maria, George, and a few others were there. I had no idea which name went with whom. Everybody had taken off their shoes, I counted ten pairs beside the door. My father-in-law's youngest brother came with a fat wife; his oldest brother had come with a wizened one. The middle brother was laid up at home in bed, but his wife was here with her brother and her—or his—eldest daughter and a son-in-law. The son-in-law was drunk as a skunk. No sooner had my father-in-law taken his coat than the man had to throw up in the bathroom, still wearing his hat and scarf. I did manage to fix two names in my mind that evening: Anastasia and Martin. Anastasia—like my late grandmother—was my father-in-law's cousin. She was about fifty years old, supposedly still a virgin, and had worked as an accountant in the cookie factory for thirty years. Martin was my father-in-law's colleague, a widowed gardener. He was supposed to make a conquest of Anastasia that New Year's Eve.

She's a bit of a cold fish, said my father-in-law, but there comes a point when they all unbutton their blouses.

Seven or eight times a year, when the relatives came, my father-in-law would flip the picture in the living room, to show the original paraputch: his parents with their six children. Mother and father sitting on the coach box, each holding a little girl. The boys were sitting in twos on the backs of the two chestnut horses. Every other day of the year the picture showed a white horse, on which sat a young man in glistening riding boots, carrying a short crop. This was my father-in-law, although not exactly. At that time he had a different name.

I danced with my husband, asking him not to spin me around, and we bobbed back and forth. When his father was present he kept his composure. I danced with the son-in-law, who after having thrown up was no longer as drunk as when he had arrived. He dragged his feet and lost a sock during the fox-trot. Martin picked it up and hung it on a branch of the chandelier. Then I danced with his father-in-law or uncle, and after that with the brothers of my father-in-law, and later with Martin. The old men had firm grips and didn't talk while they danced, I had to allow them to spin me around in silence. When my father-in-law planted himself in front of me with open arms and his tie loosened at the collar, I said:

Come and sit here at the table with me, we can talk too.

Talk, he said. Dancing keeps you young.

He had just been to the bathroom and his perfume was wafting around him. He picked out one of the liqueur cherries from a small dish perched on the corner of the table. They tasted of compote and made you drunk. I had already eaten a few too many and they had clouded my head. My father-in-law popped the cherry in his mouth and sucked the red juice from his forefinger. With his other hand he signaled me to get up. He sucked on the cherry stone and pressed his hand into the small of my back, making me aware of what he had in his trousers. I was no more curious then than I was a year later when his son reported for military service, when I was putting the towels in the cupboard and he knelt down behind me and kissed my calves.

Come on, you'll see, it will help you get over his absence.

I pressed my legs firmly together and closed the cupboard and said:

I can't stand you.

He could of course have asked why, then he would have gotten an earful. But what he said was:

There you have it. You rack your brains to come up with ways of helping the children, and this is what you get for your pains.

He wanted to take his son's place. That time when I offered myself to my father in place of the woman with the braid, it seemed both urgently necessary and quite possible. This time it was neither. I never let on to my husband and my mother-in-law, nor did they ever find out what I knew about the white horse, the Perfumed Commissar, and his change of name. He had already reinvented himself once, he had practice doing that. Hell would have frozen over before I would forget that. But I didn't make any fuss, I kept my mouth shut as usual, so that their misfortune didn't come home to roost for the whole paraputch.

By three in the morning the early hours of the New Year had already put a whole year's worth of wrinkles on our faces. The urge to grope the flesh that had married into the family gave way to yawning. The married couples, who by mutual agreement had turned a blind eye to each other's whereabouts that night, were regrouping. My mother-in-law was arguing with her husband because the crystal carafe was broken. The eldest daughter was arguing with her drunken husband because he had burnt two holes in his trousers with his cigarette. My husband was reproaching me for having toasted in the New Year with Martin before doing so with him, and for not even having noticed. The wizened wife was moaning that her husband had lost one of his gold cuff links. He showed all of us the one he still had on his right cuff, we searched the bathroom, the living room, and the hall and found old trouser buttons, coins, hairpins, perfume bottle caps, and lined them all up on the tablecloth. The youngest brother was arguing with his fat wife, because she had mislaid the car key. She emptied her handbag onto the table. A handkerchief, two aspirins, and a tiny St. Anthony made of rusting iron came tumbling out. He'll help us, she said and kissed the saint.

Why don't you eat him, said her husband, then perhaps you can work a miracle and open the car door with your finger.

Martin rested his chin on the table and gave the women's calves another ogle. Nobody took any notice, at that time of night he no longer counted as one of the family. In the glare you could make out half a finger's breadth of shiny silver in his hair, which was otherwise dyed brown.

Nobody found the cuff link, everyone stopped looking and went into the hall to put on their coats and shoes. Anastasia appeared with a rusty pair of tweezers from the bathroom. Her hands were dripping, the hair around her forehead was wet, and on her chin clung a drop of water.

How come you're drinking out of your hands, asked my mother-in-law, there are plenty of glasses.

Anastasia started crying:

I've really got to tell all of you this, that widower was absolutely horrible, the way he treated me in the bathroom, it was very rude, completely unacceptable.

The pair of tweezers lay with the other finds on the table, looking very like the small St. Anthony, but no one kissed it. Anastasia slipped on her coat and wrenched open the door.

Wait a moment, said my father-in-law, the others are all heading out as well.

I don't need anyone to see me home, she said.

The brother who had lost his cuff link pointed at her feet: You're not going in your stockings, are you.

Anastasia found the car key in her shoe.

The St. Anthony brought us luck after all, said my father-in-law to his wizened daughter-in-law.

Nobody believes in it, anyway, she said.

And then she hugged Anastasia:

Martin was just trying his luck, don't take it to heart. Who knows, something might have come of it.

By then Martin had already disappeared, no one knew how or when. He'd left his scarf hanging in the hall.

After everybody had gone, my father-in-law flipped the picture back around. My mother-in-law unhooked the sock from the chandelier, opened the windows and doors onto the street and garden. The snowy cold night blew inside. The chandelier swayed in the draft, my father-in-law's tie fluttered, as did his son's hair. Then the white horse stepped toward me from the wall, coming to fetch all these people who were so exhausted from partying on the first day of January. I retreated into the hall. My father-in-law yawned and yanked his tie over his head. His wife was bending over the carpet, picking up bread and cake crumbs and cherry stones.

The dishes have to be cleared before we can turn in, she said.

I had no intention of helping. Her husband laid his tie on the table, widening the knotted loop into a perfect circle like you see in display windows.

I said a hasty good night.

Whatever you dream about tonight will come true, he said.

That new year began with the whole paraputch talking about the missing cuff link. It isn't here in the house, it probably fell in the toilet, after all, things like that do happen. I knew better and told my husband that the gold cuff link was lying on the bedside table in his parents' jewelry box.

What are you snooping around for, he asked.

Because a cuff link can't walk, I said. The next time I peeked in the jewelry box, it had disappeared. At Easter my father-in-law was swaggering about with a gold tie pin:

From my dear wife.

She wasn't that dear a wife to him, she knew that. He had a mistress my age in the garden shop, a specialist in mites and aphids. Since no one could say her official title of Comrade Engineer for Combating Parasites in Cultivated Plants without laughing, everyone called her Comrade Louse Inspector. On Sundays my mother-in-law was happy that her husband couldn't go to the nursery. But at Easter her face was soft and mellow as dough. She couldn't get enough of looking at him, to see him so moved by his tie pin that on Sunday he didn't sneak off to the bathroom to phone his lover. My mother-in-law took a deep breath and said:

I took my old ring to the goldsmith, it was too small for me.

I felt a lump in my throat. My husband gave me a fixed stare through his keyhole eyes, the way he always did to silence me. Then I whispered in his ear:

That's half-true what your mother is saying, the cuff link alone wouldn't have been enough for your father's tie pin, her ring is gone as well.

A fat fly is buzzing in circles just above the driver's head. It settles on his arm, he tries to swat it. Then it lands on the back of his neck, he swats again. He swats himself just below his ear with a loud clap. The fly escapes and perches on the window frame. The driver tries to shoo it out the open window into the street. It drifts away, its buzzing drowned out by the rattle of the tracks. What's the matter, asks the old woman, you seem desperate. A fly, says the driver. Oh, without my glasses I can't see anything as small as that. He'll be heading your way in a minute, the driver says. Why didn't you kill it, she asks. He tried to but missed, says the man with the briefcase, he has a tram to drive, he can't go chasing flies. That would be something, a whole tram derailed because of a fly. Well, it won't be bothering me, laughs the old lady, since I shake so much. Count your blessings, says the driver. You're wrong there, she says, it's not a blessing, you'll find out soon enough when you get old. But the mosquitoes don't mind the shaking, they sure don't, and neither do the fleas. My blood is type A, that's the best one for fleas, the doctor told me. I'm AB, says the man with the briefcase. And the young lady, asks the old woman, sealing her lips in a crooked smile while she waits for the answer. O, I say. O, that's gypsy blood, says the old woman. People with type O can give blood to anybody, but they can only take from other O's. The driver slaps himself on the temple. You son of a whore, he shouts, go bother somebody else, I'm not dead yet, and I'm not a pile of shit, either. He shoos the fly in our direction. I'm not dead yet, either. I'm the youngest in the car, so when it comes to dying, I should be last in line. I'm type O too, says the driver. The fly flits around the windowpane like a floater in your eye. Its abdomen is shiny and green and large as the trembling stones dangling from the old lady's ears.

I liked to visit the workshop to see the old shoemaker because he liked to talk.

Music is my life, he would say, but I also need it here to drown out the noise the rats make. I listen to music at home too, until I fall asleep. In the old days my Vera used to sing along, day in, day out. By night she'd often be so hoarse she'd have to drink a cup of hot tea with honey.

Every summer his wife would plant dahlias along the wire fence that caught the morning sun.

She sure had a green thumb, my Vera, he said, she got everything to bloom. But the last summer she was home, her dahlias started sprouting strange leaves—leaves that really belonged on fritillarias, zinnias, delphiniums, and phlox. The same thing happened when the dahlias began to flower, each single stem seemed to have everything imaginable. The dahlias looked absolutely amazing, but they were a little crazy too. People would stop at the fence to look. Before the flowers started to fade, my daughter dug them all up so the wind wouldn't scatter the crazy seeds around. Vera had always been a pretty quiet person, but after those dahlias bloomed she scarcely said a word. Physically she was fit as a fiddle but she wasn't much use around the house, so my daughter sent her out shopping every day. Vera'd come back with beans instead of potatoes, vinegar instead of fizzy water, matches instead of toilet paper. When Vera didn't get any better, my daughter wrote out a shopping list for her. My poor forgetful Vera showed the list to the people in the shop, but she still came home with shoelaces instead of toothpaste, or thumbtacks instead of cigarettes. So my daughter went straight down to the shop. The shop assistant and the cashier remembered the lady with the list perfectly. No, they said, she hadn't bought any shoelaces or thumbtacks, just toothpaste and cigarettes, exactly as it said on the list. Besides, we don't even have any shoelaces, they've been on order for weeks but haven't been delivered yet. And we don't carry thumbtacks at all. From that point on, Vera was only allowed out for an hour's walk every morning. But she started coming back with a handbag that belonged to someone else. Usually there was an I.D. card inside, so my daughter could return the bag to its proper owner and recover her mother's. Then one day we weren't able to track down Vera's own purse, and meanwhile she was bringing home more and more handbags belonging to other women, so after that she could go out only if she left the house with nothing in her hands and came back with nothing. But then she'd come back wearing a hat instead of her headscarf. During the winter we couldn't let her out because of the cold, but the following spring Vera went out three times wearing a dress and showed up all out of breath dressed in a skirt and blouse. At that point I agreed to put her in a mental home. There's not a clothing store anywhere in the neighborhood, said the old shoemaker, so she definitely wasn't stealing. One thing's for sure, Vera would never have stolen anything. Even the people in the neighborhood said that much. Out on the street she always looked fairly normal. Almost too self-effacing, people said. She never returned their greetings, though; she'd just pass by and say:

I left the rice on, so I've got to run.

The old shoemaker pinched the corners of his mouth with his thumb and index finger. But now it doesn't matter anymore. It's neither here nor there, like so much in life.

For my part, I told the old shoemaker about my dead grandmother, and that after my father died my grandfather had said that life was just the farty sputter of a lantern, not even worth the bother of putting your shoes on.

He's right about that, the old man said, your grandfather must be a bit of a philosopher, you can't be dumb and come up with something like that.

Then he pointed to the boards where shoes were hanging on every nail:

But look there. When it comes to shoes, I have to see things a little differently, else I wouldn't have any bread to eat.

Stretched out under his lips, the skin between the old man's thumb and index finger, yellowed from the leather wax, looked like webbing from a duck's foot.

My Vera, at least she wound up that way by herself. But there are two young women in the mental home with her who lost their wits after what the police did to them. These women hadn't done anything, either—one swiped a little candle wax from the factory, the other took a sack of corncobs that was lying in a field. Now, you tell me, what kind of crime is that.

The young shoemaker said: I don't have any rubber or any leather for the soles. He slid his hands into Paul's sandals as if they were mittens, turned them upside down, and stared at the blackberry that was crushed into the sole. His teeth stuck out as his mouth opened and closed; in my thoughts I was somewhere else. The boy who made the dust snakes was dead because I didn't stay to play with him. My father died because he didn't want to go on hiding from me. My grandfather, because I had lied about his death. And Lilli, because I had said that her officer's stomach was round as a ball, like the setting sun. Now the old shoemaker had died because I had danced my fill of the world. The young man with the crooked mouth wrapped the sandals back inside the newspaper.

Check in ten days and we'll see what's what. I could already see what was what. I nodded and left.

Outside the wind was flying through the street, clusters of little green peas were dropping from the lindens. Each cluster had a small leathery wing—that had nothing to do with the sawtoothed, heart-shaped leaves on the boughs. A sofa of white clouds was floating high in the evening summer sky. A woman slipped out of the pharmacy carrying a small vial. The contents, the rubber stopper, and the woman's thumb were the color of indigo. I asked her for the time. The woman said:

It's about half past eight.

I had wanted to do something for Paul, not in ten days' time, as the young shoemaker suggested, but that very day, between seven and just about half past eight. I had failed. The pharmacist was sitting in the window next to a stack of tiny boxes with Chinese writing on them, barefoot, her back to the street. Each box was filled so tight you couldn't have squeezed a coat button inside. They looked like those condom wrappers that had the word Butterfly printed next to all the Chinese characters. Lilli had once said:

The Chinese are crafty bastards. They export the good rubbers to America for the Chinese in New York's Chinatown. The ones with the holes they send to us and the Bulgarians.

Each of the boxes was jammed with wads of cotton wool, and inside each was one glass eye. The pharmacist was arranging the eyes in a row along the bare wood of the windowsill: light brown, dark brown, green flecked, light blue, and dark blue. The light brown eyes would have been right for Paul; I counted them. Then I counted my own dark brown ones. There were more of Paul's. Behind the window, in the deep red glow of the sun, the pharmacist started on her second row. She was sitting in an aquarium. I tapped on the window, she turned her head, brushed the hair from her forehead, and kept going. Her eyes were gray flecked with green.

The white sofa in the sky, the pharmacist in the aquarium, the linden seeds, Paul's sandals like mittens on the young shoemaker's hands, Mulberry Street lined with acacias—after the old shoemaker died everything seemed out of control. The wind might not have managed to scatter the crazy dahlia seeds, but it had sown a feeling of vertigo among the shoelaces and toothpaste, cigarettes and thumbtacks, headscarf and hat. And now blindness was being peddled on this red evening in the city, with glass eyes for everyone. But death comes knocking especially for those who think they can dance their fill of the world in order to be happy. Yes, that's the way we'd like it: we'd wear the crown and have our fill of the world. But isn't it the other way around, that the world has its fill of us, and not we of it.

Not that everybody is included in this us. Not everyone goes mad, just as not everyone gets summoned. Lilli wasn't summoned, although for weeks after the first notes I was convinced she would be. I wanted to prepare her for the feeling you get at your first interrogation, the way the roof of your mouth rises up and glues itself onto your brain. That's how it feels the second time as well, and every time after that, but in time you stop being frightened. Lilli wasn't worried.

I've never even seen your notes.

As if that was a reason not to be summoned. As if those who

know nothing except how fear can set your heart racing weren't the easiest prey. With the roof of your mouth inside your brain you give yourself away. They'd probably questioned Nelu and the girls from the packing hall about me. Nelu hated me, and the girls didn't know me well enough to care. I didn't care about them, either, but the fact that their words froze in their throats the minute a door in the corridor was cracked open did not bode well.

Lilli was right, she was never summoned. That was lucky, even though she could have stood up for me. She couldn't have stood up for herself. The only thing Lilli asked me about the interrogations was:

How old is your major.

What's that supposed to mean—my major, I said, and I pretended he was ten years younger than he really was.

About forty.

Oh, heavens, said Lilli, once she had ruled him out for herself. I knew for a fact that Albu would have started feeling Lilli up the very first time. She would have gone along or turned him away, in either case he would have exacted some fearful revenge. A few days after that conversation, Lilli mentioned that her parents had had a fight. Her mother didn't want to let her stepfather out of the house. The reason was a rendezvous, but not with a woman. It was about a newsstand in the park, where her stepfather was supposed to show up at five in the afternoon. Lilli's mother said:

Today you're staying home for once. I'll call the switchboard and tell them you're sick. With all the kids crawling around the city, you ought to put your foot down, let them find someone younger.

She blocked his way. Lilli's stepfather took his wallet and shoved her aside:

Where'd you get that idea—put my foot down, and how pray tell am I going to do that. You act big at home all right, he shouted, but at the market you're pretty quick to shove the melon at me to hold so that camel of a lieutenant can kiss your hand. And then you even say to him—imagine, the lady saying to the man—The honor's mine. Here you come on so brave and courageous, but when someone like that shows up, you're so scared you can't even swallow your own spit. Better go take your heart pills instead.

I was wondering about the games that life plays, and on my way back from the shoemaker I went through all the possible ways of getting fed up with the world. The first and the best: don't get summoned and don't go mad, like most people. The second possibility: don't get summoned, but do lose your mind, like the shoemaker's wife and Frau Micu who lives downstairs by the main entrance. The third: do get summoned and do go mad, like the two women in the mental home. Or else the fourth: get summoned but don't go mad, like Paul and myself. Not particularly good, but in our case the best option. A squashed plum was lying on the pavement, the wasps were eating their fill, the newly hatched ones as well as the older wasps. What must it be like when a whole family can fit on a single plum. The sun was being pulled out of the city into the fields. At first glance its makeup looked a little too garish, especially for the hour; at second glance it appeared to have been shot—red as a bed of poppies, Lilli's officer had said. Yes, that's the fifth possibility: to be very young, and unbelievably beautiful, and not insane, but dead. You don't have to be named Lilli to be dead.

I carried the worn-out sandals back home. The red car was no longer parked on the sidewalk. Looking at the bare asphalt you couldn't even tell it had been there, and the cigarette butts lying on the ground had no idea what had happened. Cats were rummaging through the garbage for something to eat before night revoked all territorial boundaries and strange cats with a green light in their eyes would show up and help themselves, before the wails of hunger and the howls of coupling became one. Compared with this summer evening, my face was cool. From the apartment block next door I heard a shattering of dishes: someone had dropped something. People were eating. The rising moon was half full, two faces were beginning to peek through—a goat's and a dog's. The moon would have to choose which face was better suited for this night, time was pressing. Flowers were flowing out of window boxes on the second story. A whirligig was spinning and whirring in the petunias, by the time the moon chose its face they would have been given water for growing. I'd done a lot that day, and despite the failures I had managed to hit upon the best option for Paul and me:

Neither one of us will go mad.

My ass-backward happiness was banging at my temples, demanding to get in, I wasn't the dumbest woman in the world. The shops had already closed, and there was a light on in our kitchen window. Paul would be waiting with two pairs of new shoes, ready to ask which he should wear and which he should put in his tool cabinet. He should wear whichever pair looks better. Of course he might pick the ones I think are uglier, he doesn't always see what I see, just like with the photo of Lilli. It's the only picture I have of her, and I confess I look at it often. I look at it and talk about her beauty, everyone agrees on that, but Paul frowns.

What is it about her that's supposed to have been so beautiful, I prefer you, and I'm not just saying that. The most beautiful thing about her is that you liked her so much.

It's hard to keep a straight face when he says that, and I've often had to say:

Paul, you have a good heart but bad taste.

Nevertheless, that night, while Paul was trying on his shoes, I intended to tell him about the glass eyes in the pharmacy window and about the option of not going mad, and most of all that I was not the dumbest woman in the world.

A motorcycle was parked outside our apartment house. The mirror and headlight had been torn off it, the seat had been slashed and the handlebars and pedals bent out of shape. It was Paul's red Java, I felt the goose bumps break out on my scalp. As I was waiting for the elevator I felt as though I'd left my body and been parceled out among the mailboxes fixed to the wall. But the mailboxes stayed on the wall when the elevator door opened, and it was I who got in, the dumbest woman in the world.

As Paul was riding back from the shop, a gray truck had pulled up behind him, it never left his rearview mirror. Paul pulled over to let it pass. There wasn't much traffic. He was driving quite slowly, the truck pulled up close to him, so close on the roundabout that it seemed the driver wanted to ram right into the Java. Then the motorbike flew up, and Paul went hurtling through the air, without his bike, and then came falling down like deadwood from a tree. When he dared open his eyes, he saw grass and heard voices. He looked around and saw shoes, pants, skirts, and, very high up, faces. Paul asked:

Where's the bike.

It was lying by the curb.

Where's the truck.

No one had seen it.

Where are my shoes.

On your feet, said an old man in shorts.

122

The ones that were in the bag on the handlebars, where are they.

Good God Almighty, said the old man, it's a miracle you still have all your teeth, and now you want shoes. You have a guardian angel, isn't that enough for you.

My guardian angel's driving that gray truck, said Paul, where did it go.

What truck. You better stop speeding around on that thing.

The legs sticking out of the short pants were like marble, heavily veined and hairless. When the crowd that had gathered saw that Paul still had all his teeth and was coherent, it dispersed. The old man helped him to get up and stand the motorbike upright. Then he handed Paul his handkerchief:

At least wipe the blood off your chin.

Did you see the gray truck, asked Paul.

I saw several.

Did you catch the number.

Fate doesn't have a number.

But trucks do.

Stick with fate, said the old man, otherwise your guardian angel might take offense.

Meanwhile Paul had wiped the blood from his chin with the freshly ironed handkerchief.

Now Paul was lying on the bed in the dark room. After describing the accident he asked me:

Are you supposed to return a dirty handkerchief, or do you keep it.

I shrugged. The more Paul talked about the old man, the less I thought his presence there was just coincidence. After Paul had sidetracked the conversation into handkerchief etiquette, he took a second detour.

The fact that somebody stole another pair of shoes from me bothers me more than the accident.

I looked out the window, the street lay far below, silent, deserted, and the moon had chosen the goat's face. If the moon hadn't made a mistake, the face would last for the night. Halfway out of the window, I said:

The last time I was summoned, Albu smiled a little as he was kissing my hand: You and your husband drive down to the river quite often, don't you, and accidents do happen on the roads.

The goat's face was lurking overhead, and the sky was swirling by, and when I stopped looking outside the whole room was reeling. Maybe people are right to keep asking if I'm not afraid the leaning tower might collapse.

Paul had turned the light on:

How come you didn't tell me this before.

Because I didn't believe it. Albu was just casting about and settled on an accident. Bloodshot eyes, wrinkled gums, cold hands had all served their turn. Or so I thought.

Outside the night was black and inside it was light, we'd been talking in the dark so long we hadn't even looked at the wounds on Paul's forehead, chin, wrists, knees, and elbows. They were caked with dirt and dried blood. I got some cotton wool and alcohol from the bathroom. I wanted to put my arms around Paul but didn't dare, his scrapes would have hurt even more, on the outside, and nothing would have helped on the inside. He ran his fingers through his hair and then screwed up his face as if even that hurt.

Leave me alone, he said.

Paul dabbed quickly and firmly at the wounds on his knees, elbows, and knuckles. The stinging brought tears to his eyes, he wiped them with the inside of his arm, just before the tears clouded his vision completely. He let me dab at his forehead and chin, because he didn't want to look in the mirror. My dabs were different, more hesitant, he gave a pained laugh, and in the end I said:

What are you trying to prove. If something hurts you should scream.

And he did scream, though what he really said was:

Take a good look at my face and you'll see exactly what you've been keeping from me.

He grabbed me by the throat and squeezed like a pair of pliers. And I did what he wanted me to do, I stared right at him, my eyes bulging. The wound I had cleaned on his chin was gleaming raw, it stuck in my eye like a spat-out mouthful of watermelon. But then I saw my first husband's suitcase standing on the bridge. At that point I could have said, should have said, should have been able to say:

Nobody's ever going to treat me like that again, in the hatred born of love, do you understand, never again, as long as I live. Instead of which I pulled his hands away from my neck. Once you start backing down, you end up with your head over the railing. Hopefully I won't have to go through the same thing all over. Hopefully I won't ever feel as contemptible in Paul's eyes as my first husband had felt in mine.

Beginning tomorrow we'll travel by bus and tram, said Paul. The jokers will have a harder time of it.

He stumbled into the kitchen. The refrigerator door opened, closed, there was a glugging sound as Paul drank out of a bottle, I hoped it wasn't brandy, but it certainly wasn't water. A glass came clinking out of a shelf and landed on the table. I heard it being filled, it wasn't one of the big ones. He drank noisily, and I waited. The glass didn't return to the table, nor was a chair pulled out for sitting. Paul was standing in the kitchen, holding the glass in one of his grazed hands. And if the moon had wandered over there, the face of the goat would be looking helplessly at him, and his wounded face would be looking back.

Perched on the door frame was a mosquito, standing out in the light like a brooch. It was off its guard, I could have killed it. As soon as we turned out the light it would sing and feed until it was all fed up. This was a lucky night; it didn't even have to bite, it could simply suck up the blood with its proboscis. Unfortunately it had a discerning nose, it would prefer me, Paul's blood probably reeked too much of brandy for its taste.

There was something fishy about that old man with the handkerchief, Paul shouted from the kitchen. He's probably laughing himself shitless. I was happy just to be alive, I didn't catch on, I barely understood what was happening.

The brandy, or the goat's face, had taken the shock out of Paul, but the mosquito hadn't done the same for me. I asked:

Can you see the moon through the kitchen window.

⌐ The next morning the sun came groping into our bed, two insect bites were itching on my arm, and one on my forehead ⌊and one on my cheek. The night before, Paul had been drugged asleep by the brandy, and I had been dragged asleep by a weariness that was faster than the mosquito. I had stopped asking myself questions before going to sleep, questions about how to get through the days, since I didn't know the answer. What I did know was that questions like that could make you forget how to sleep. The first week after the business with the notes, when I was summoned for three days in a row, I couldn't sleep a wink. My nerves were razor wire. My body shed weight, it was nothing but taut skin and hollow bones. When I was running around town I had to be careful that I didn't just turn into smoke and leave my body, the way my breath did in winter, or that I didn't swallow myself when I yawned. The frozen waste inside me was gaping far wider than I could open my mouth. I began to feel I was being swept along by something lighter than myself, I even began to take pleasure in the sensation, the more numb I grew within. On the other hand, I was afraid that all the specters would come to seem even more attractive, and that I wouldn't lift a finger to stop them or help myself get back. On the third day, as I was heading home from Albu, I found myself walking to the park. I lay with my face in the grass, unable to feel a thing. I couldn't have cared less if I'd been lying below the grass, dead, I would have welcomed it, and at the same time I liked living so damned much. I wanted to have a good cry and instead wound up laughing myself silly. Good thing the earth sounds so dull and hollow, I laughed until I was tired. When I stood up I was feeling more vain than I had been for a long time: I fixed my dress, tidied my hair, looked to see whether there were any blades of grass stuck in my shoes, whether my hands had turned green and my fingernails dirty. Only then did I leave the park, stepping from a green room onto the sidewalk. At that moment I heard something rustling in my left ear, a beetle had crawled inside. The buzzing was loud and clear, my whole head was echoing with the sound of stilts clattering in an empty hall.

I was right, the mosquito preferred me, and I had yielded, since it was imperative for Paul and me not to bother each other. I should have told the mosquito not to bite my face. In the light of day the scabs on Paul's forehead and chin looked like a clogged sieve, where you couldn't tell what was supposed to stay in and what should pass through.

My cuts were burning last night, Paul said, my mouth was all dried out, I had to keep going to the window so as not to suffocate.

He rubbed his eyes. Traffic could be heard in the street with the shops, soon bottles had started clinking. I crossed to the window: a delivery truck had pulled up out back, and the red car was parked on the sidewalk in the same place as yesterday, only no one was inside. It was just sitting there in the sun, completely empty. To ask what it was doing there would have been as senseless as asking the same thing of the trees, the clouds, or the rooftops. I was just about ready to accept the idea that the unoccupied car should simply be where it was. Up here in the flat Paul's steps were making the floor creak, while down below on the sidewalk a woman walked into her own shadow. The summer clouds were bright and high, or, rather, soft and close, while Paul and I seemed as if we'd been stored on the wrong shelf, too tired, placed too high off the ground. Neither of us really wanted to stave off defeat—I don't even think Paul did. Our misfortune went on and on, weighing us down. Happiness had become a liability, and my ass-backward luck a kind of trap. If we tried to protect each other, it would come to nothing. Just as when Paul joined me at the window and I ran the tip of my finger across his chin to keep him from sticking his head out. He sensed the restraint in my affection and leaned outside: he saw the red car. Tenderness has its own meshes, whenever I attempt to spin threads like a spider I get stuck in my own web, in so many little lumpy balls. I yielded the window to Paul, he didn't think the unoccupied red car was worth more than a passing curse. But then he went downstairs in his slippers, without saying a word, and hauled the Java up in the elevator. We dragged the motorcycle into the apartment. And two days later, on Sunday, Paul pushed it along Mulberry Street to the flea market.

I had decided to stay home. I couldn't go to Mulberry Street without visiting Lilli's grave and looking for the shoemaker's. And that could have taken some time. I didn't like visiting Lilli's grave. If it had been just the two of us I could have handled it—but not those red flowers too, right there on her grave. My father-in-law had called them haemanthus. At the market they were called blood lilies. For me, they were the flowers of flesh. Red stems, leaves, blooms, each plant to its very tips was a handful of ragged flesh. Lilli was feeding them, and I would stand at the foot of the grave and put my finger in my mouth to keep my teeth from chattering. After Paul's accident, nothing could induce me to visit any grave on earth. And what was more, I still wanted to keep the Java, even if it was no longer roadworthy.

Our love had come full circle. We had first met at the flea market, and the motorbike had been there. Paul hadn't been to the flea market since; now he was going there to sell his Java. Paul said:

If we hold on to the bike, we'll never get rid of this whole nasty business.

Whether or not that was true, I wanted to keep it in the apartment because it was the accident that was nasty, not the Java. And just as nasty as that was the image of Paul sitting there in the dust of the flea market, every bit as battered and bruised as his bike. I said:

You can't go there with that scab on your face.

Paul made light of it:

Who knows, maybe your beach ball will turn up again.

What did turn up again was the old man with the marbled

legs. Spic-and-span in his Sunday best, with a breezy straw hat and a silk tie. And Paul sold him the Java and decided that the old man couldn't have been from the secret police, otherwise he wouldn't have offered more than anybody else. I'm not so sure.

Late that evening Paul came home from the flea market drunk. He got some sausage out of the fridge and bread from the cupboard. Every time he picked up a piece to eat, he asked:

What's that.

Sausage, I said.

And that.

Tomato.

And what on earth is that.

Bread.

And what's that.

Salt and a knife. The other thing is a fork.

As he chewed, Paul looked across at me, as if he had to find me.

Sausage, tomato, salt, and bread, he said. But you're here too.

And where have you been, I asked.

He pointed to his chest with the knife handle:

In my shirt and right with you.

He dropped a crust of bread into his shirt pocket:

If I'm arrested anytime soon . . . or if you're . . . His chewed-up food dragged the words down into his throat. After eating, he put the cutlery in the sink and the bread in the drawer and wiped the crumbs from the table:

We should clean up in case we have an unexpected visitor today.

A few minutes later he came into the bedroom and sat down next to me on the edge of the bed:

Aren't we going to eat today.

But you just had something.

When.

Five minutes ago.

What did I eat.

I listed everything again.

He nodded.

So the man is full, he said.

At that I nodded.

It was good he didn't say *your man*. If he wanted to drink all the money he got for the Java, that was entirely his own business. I didn't even want to know how much he got. I'd never again be literally struck dumb with happiness when we were out for a ride, the sky would never again start flying, and never again would I hold on tight to Paul's ribs—that was entirely my own business, as was the fact that we didn't use the money to go to the restaurant by the game preserve, like we had after we first met at the flea market. Paul had the accident without me, his motorcycle was finished, perhaps he was trying to spare us both the feeling of a wake. For Paul it was a question of wiping away the accident, as he had wiped away the bread crumbs from the kitchen table. Just as I had wanted to wipe everything away after I separated from my first husband.

Back then I had gone to the flea market to rid myself of all the things that reminded me of him. Where the wedding ring was concerned, it was a matter of the money—I had debts. Paul was standing next to me, selling homemade television aerials designed to pick up stations from Belgrade and Budapest. The aerials were officially prohibited, but they were tolerated and could be seen on lots of roofs around the city. Here at the flea market, splayed out on Paul's blue tarp that the wind kept tearing at, they looked like antlers. I took off my shoes and used them to anchor the newspaper on which I had laid out the items I was trying to sell. My feet got dirty, and that made me unhappy, just as it had when I played with the boy they put to sleep and his dust snakes swirling between the avenue and the bread factory. The people who shuffled by might just as well have sold the clothes off their back and wrapped themselves in any old rags they could pick up off the ground. Only soldiers and policemen would have stood out, because there were no uniforms lying on the ground. Not a single tree, not one blade of grass, just a mass of ragged people and a poor man's summer in the whirling dust. And there I was, selling gold.

For my woolen scarf I could have gotten three times the price I was paid. The plastic bangles and brooches, my beach hat, and the beach ball would never have brought in more than a little change. In my short, narrow skirt, with my wedding ring dangling to the ground from my wrist on a length of string, I felt doubly sly—part black marketeer fallen on hard times who shows a little skin to make her goods more attractive, part rouge-cheeked whore who manages to clean out her client's wallet during sex. A little depravity would have fit right in with the place, would have guaranteed a quick killing. I liked imagining myself depraved and desirable. I crooked my right leg a little, rested my right heel on my left foot, ran my fingers through my bangs, and gave provocative, seductive looks for all I was worth. But I was convinced that my short skirt spoiled things because of my bandy legs, that my neck wasn't a true milky-white, and that my eyes didn't have that petulant edge that drives men wild when a woman glances up from beneath her lashes. The most suggestive thing about me was the whirling dust. In fact, I didn't even know what the ring weighed, nor the going price of gold. I belonged to the ring and not the other way around. Please have pity on this poor silly goose—I could have pulled that off more easily. But pity would have been out of place here.

An old man hefted the ring and examined the hallmark with a magnifying glass.

It's gold, what else would it be, I said.

What are you asking, two thousand, huh.

I'm not sure I want to sell it.

Two thousand one hundred, come on, let's call it a deal.

That's easy for you to say.

All right, I'll take another walk around.

And how long will that be.

Say, a quarter of an hour.

By that time the ring'll be gone.

Then hand it over.

Not so fast.

How much do you want.

Do you have the money on you.

Jesus Christ Almighty, you expect me to wave it about in the air.

What's your top offer.

Two thousand two hundred, hmm. You want to sell, or would you rather go sit on Granddaddy's lap.

I'll think about it.

What's a little pussycat like you hunting out here, anyway, he shouted.

I stared right past him, he put away his magnifying glass, but hesitated to leave. He would rather have made a deal than have nothing to show for his trip to the market. He stood before me in the dust wearing a freshly ironed, blue-striped shirt, hardly somebody's granddad whose lap you could go sit on. His stomach, hands, and temples were the same as Lilli's officer. Today the sun, which was as round as a ball, was wrapped in cotton wool.

Paul had a lot of takers, he was showing off his aerials and handing out leaflets explaining how to aim them to pick up Belgrade and Budapest. I crouched down and my skirt slid right up, I tugged at it in vain. The old man was right, I was looking up at Paul the way a cat eyes a person. Paul's motorbike was beside him, occasionally someone would bump into it. I would flinch, expecting to see it keel over, and see my father die all over again. Paul was asking two thousand lei for an aerial and getting half that. He bowed to a young married couple who found even that price too high:

Then go on, point the antennas of your hearts toward Bucharest, and much good may it do you.

He was a good salesman, he knew how to be cheeky without offending, I on the other hand, gave my beach hat to the first gap-toothed, doubled-chinned woman who came along, and when I sold the bracelets it was to girls with hairy arms and I took whatever they offered. In the factory the pay packets appeared on the table twice a month as if by magic, mail from an unknown hand. Everybody pocketed the money and threw away the envelope without checking. There was nothing to do about how much the envelope contained, you just went on in your quiet and unprotesting way. I was desperately in need of money, but I didn't know how to talk up the things I wanted to get rid of, nor did I know how to make money by using my wits.

Next to the fence enclosing the market was a broken concrete pipe. At one end a man sat pouring red wine from a tin container into an old frosted-glass lamp globe, which he then drained. At the other end a man was affectionately kissing the hair of a child who was sitting in his lap. Between them some rusty wire stuck out of a crack in the pipe. In my mind I switched the three of us around, so that the man with the child was drinking from the glass globe—even I could do that. Then

the man with the tin container had to kiss the child, but he discovered he had forgotten how—while someone like me, with a
wedding ring dangling from a piece of string, never knew how
in the first place. And either one of the men would have sold
the ring more quickly than I could. The dust was swirling the
ground up to the sky, the day was out of joint. The only customer for the last two remaining television aerials at that
moment was the wind. Paul screwed up his eyes.

Is that your wedding ring.

I don't know whether my feeble nod gave me away or
whether he had long since figured out I was a little pussycat out
hunting.

Ask for six thousand, he said, and don't go below five.

A fly settled on my big toe and stung me, I watched it from
the corner of my eye and felt ashamed to kill it because I had to
say straight out:

My marriage wasn't worth that much.

Who says, you or your husband, asked Paul.

Then I had to go to the toilet, two small wooden cabins at
the far end of the flea market.

Leave the ring here, said Paul.

The fact that he even took the trouble, that he even thought
about me at all. He untied the string from my wrist, I stretched
out my arm and looked away the way children do when they're
being undressed. But where my skin was thinnest I could feel
my pulse practically leaping out at him. His fingers were busy
with the knot but my interest was all in the touching. After he
had untied me, I took my time putting on my shoes. Paul was
wearing my wedding ring on his little finger, he stretched his
hand out over the television aerials, dangling the string and
making up a singsong rhyme:

A kiss on the hand
and a golden band
can rob you of your senses.

It was comic, but he was performing it seriously, a real showman, and people stopped. I laughed as I walked away down the long rows. Outside the fence, at the end of the market, was the uneasy calm of an abandoned building site. Bindweed, knotgrass, and morning glories were crawling among the cranes, pipes, and crumbled cement. The finger I had been thinking of for some time was not the ring finger.

Right after the kiss on my hand, when I was summoned the second time after the notes, the only thing I could think of was that I had to go to the toilet. Albu said:

But of course. Down the corridor to the left, the next to last door. But leave your handbag here.

I went down the corridor to the left, I didn't want to rush, but neither did I want to overdo things by taking too long. Two doors away a telephone was ringing, and it was still ringing later when I returned, no one was answering it. In the inner courtyard there were two pumps, for diesel and gasoline, and one for water. Two gray trucks, a bus with green curtains, a minibus, a blue car, a white one. And two red ones. At the end of the corridor, behind a door, someone was crying. On the sink was a cake of soap with two black hairs stuck to it, below in the trash can was a bloody handkerchief. It was then I felt my heart stick in my throat, my footsteps quickened. No doubt I came back sooner than was necessary.

Now the tram driver is ringing his bell, there's a dog running right across the road, a rangy, splotchy creature, all skin and bones, holding his tail between his legs, and his paws are matted with half-dried mud. God knows where he found mud in this heat. His muzzle is dripping with foam, it's no point even bothering with the bell, the dog would be better off dead, he could finally stretch out and rest. You see more and more dogs like that, says the young man standing by the door. The man with the briefcase nods: And if they bite you, that's it, you're through, you barely have enough time left to send for the priest and confess. It happened to a boy on my street. He was foaming at the mouth just like that dog, nothing to be done about it, rabies, finished. The old woman with the shaky head says: It's that artificial fertilizer they're putting on the fields, that's why all the dogs are turning into runts. They fertilize like mad, but the only things that actually grow are fat rats, deformed birds, and razor grass. Everything else is godforsaken and stunted. Tell me, what am I supposed to do if a dog like that comes after me, at least you young folks can still run. And just a few years back I was still the fastest thing on two legs. My son used to say: You're like a whirlwind, take it easy. Running away is the wrong thing to do, the young man says. If a dog like that comes at you, you have to stand still and act absolutely sure of yourself, look the beast square in the eye, like you're trying to hypnotize it. That's if your eyes are good, but not if you wear glasses, the old woman laughs. Heavens, without my glasses I can't tell his head from his tail. Maybe it works if you look him square in the tail, the driver laughs, anyway it'd be worth a try. A while back in the park I saw a bird with three feet, the old woman says, I swear I'm not making it up, I was wearing my glasses. I couldn't believe it, so I asked two youngsters if it was real. And it was. How's your headache, the man with the briefcase asks. Bad, the old woman says, it's easy enough for your mind to forget the years you've lived through, they're over and

137

done with, but your eyes, your feet, your gallbladder, they don't forget, and it all starts to catch up with you. The driver unbuttons his shirt from top to bottom. Next stop is the marketplace, he says, we'll be there in a moment.

So you feel drawn to the south, Albu said. We've got pigeons and a fountain in front of the opera house here too. But girls like you want orange trees, and where do they end up, huh, tell me, where do they end up. In a sleazy hotel with rooms let by the hour, with bank robbers wearing fat gold chains and platform shoes, pimps with pockmarked faces and long teeth and—he held up the nibbled pencil—pricks no bigger than that.

So maybe Albu's own prick is like that and the pencil stub serves as a measure of the world.

What am I taking away from this country by going to another, I asked.

The Major rolled the stub between his thumb and index finger. He spoke gently, as if he was talking to himself and I wasn't meant to hear: People who don't love their homeland can't understand. And people not smart enough to think have no choice but to feel.

Lilli attached great importance to the hands of her men. She wouldn't have been able to watch those slender fingers rolling the pencil without drawing Albu's hand closer to her. But whatever might have happened within these walls, Lilli would not have forgotten how irresistible she was, and she would have summoned him to her—outside, somewhere in town, and there she would have had him. A floor, a bench, some patch of grass—there's always somewhere to lie down if your heart is being torn apart with need. Albu would have dropped all ranks and titles and thrown his reason to the wind just for a chance to prowl around Lilli's beautiful flesh. And when he resumed being a major back at his large desk, he himself would have avoided strangers out of fear, and this fear would have caused him to comb out his hair and think up plausible excuses he could tell his boss. He would have to lie, just like I do, in a tousled state of fear. That would serve him right. Of course, I wouldn't have understood Lilli when she would have told me what happened, looking at me with those plum-blue eyes that grew darker still for older men. She would have unpeeled a little of the secret, but kept the core silent, with that famous tobacco flower in her face. We would have hurt each other, I would have hurt her and she would have hurt me. But to the outsider seeing us together, we would simply have been sitting comfortably in a café. Or we would be out for a walk.

We will never get through at this rate, Albu said.

To clarify the facts of the case, I was supposed to write down every Italian I knew. I was sick and tired of the facts of the case, it was almost evening, I didn't know any Italians and said so, in vain. He charged about and yelled:

You're lying.

And yet he acted as if he knew everything. A man like him must have realized I wasn't lying. So he forced me to keep at it, to follow his facts of the case, until he went off duty. He stretched his legs, loosened his tie, tossed back his head. He combed his hair nervously, checked if there were any hairs in the comb, returned it to his rear pants pocket. He banged his fist on the table and stood in front of me. He shoved my face down against the blank paper, pulled me up from my chair by the ear, that burned like fire. Then he ran his hand into my hair above the temple, twisted my hair around his index finger, and yanked me, as if by a tassel, around the office, over to the window, and back to the chair. And when I was sitting down facing the paper, I wrote:

Marcello.

I was biting my lips, I couldn't think of any other name apart from Mastroianni and Mussolini, and those were names he knew as well.

I don't know his last name.

And where did you meet this Marcello.

At the seashore.

The sea where.

Constantsa.

What were you doing there.

Looking for the harbor.

The harbor's full of shit. So what about this Marcello.

He came off a boat.

What was the boat's name.

I didn't see it.

You didn't see the boat, he said, but you saw his uniform.

He was wearing regular summer clothes.

But you could smell he was a sailor.

He told me he was.

Albu knew I was lying, he was forcing me to, and I believed my own lies out of sheer desolation. Then he opened the drawer and peeked inside as he put away the pencil. As he closed the drawer he said:

Go home and think about it. I'll see you tomorrow at ten. Ten sharp, don't forget. After all, we've still got the notes for France and Sweden. You probably had accomplices with those, this is a serious business. Ten sharp.

That was the first time I'd heard anything about notes meant for France. Had Nelu lied to him, or had he actually written another whole set of notes, or was it a girl from the packing hall. Did Albu have them in his drawer and was he going to show them to me tomorrow. Or was he telling me something he'd made up just before letting me go, something designed to drive me crazy by tomorrow morning. My tongue grew cold, is this never going to end.

When I stepped outside everything was preparing for the night, the sun had already spread itself red across the sky, every shadow in town had lain down. Inside my head was buzzing with thoughts, on top my scalp felt loose, and over my scalp my hair was being blown by the wind. Wind is made for flying, traffic lights for flashing, cars for driving, trees for standing. Does any of this really mean anything, or is it just there for you to wonder about. My tongue was licking at my brain, it tasted sickly sweet, I saw a food stand and imagined either that I was hungry or that I ought to be. I asked for a piece of poppy-seed cake, rummaged in my bag for my wallet, and felt some hard piece of paper that didn't belong to me. I walked a few yards to a bench, put the cake down on my lap, and took out a little package. It was wrapped in yellow-gray paper, the ends were firmly twisted as if around a piece of candy, there was something hard inside. I opened the little packet and strained my eyes to see what it was. What I saw was not a cigarette or a twig, it wasn't a parsnip, and it wasn't a bird's claw, it was a finger with a bluish-black nail. I quickly stuffed it back in my bag. Sunlight came slanting through the gaps between the boards in back of the food stand, I held the poppy-seed cake in front of my mouth as if I were feeding a sick person. The kiosk came lurching toward me, driven forward by the rays of light. I chewed slowly, I felt the sugar crunching all the way up inside my forehead, I wasn't thinking of anything; actually, it was as though all of a sudden nothing mattered to me anymore. After all, I was healthy, while the cake was being eaten by some poor invalid who felt she had to swallow something to stay alive. And I convinced this other person that she liked the taste, until the poppy-seed cake had completely vanished from my hand. Then I rewrapped the finger in the paper and retwisted the ends. I was completely undone. Death, with whom we flirt now and then just to keep it at bay, was advancing, checking for an available time and date—perhaps one was already circled in Albu's diary. The food stand stayed where it was, the bench was empty, I started walking and walking. I saw different deaths, lean and fat, with bald spots or full heads of hair, parted or fringed, all combing the town to find my date. I saw shirts buttoned and open, long and short trousers, sandals and shoes, paper bags, purses, mesh bags, empty hands. Other people out walking gave their assistance in many different ways to help death find my date.

I went up to five lampposts and looked inside the trash bins, two were half-empty. People toss trash away quickly and carelessly. The nail of the finger was black, its skin was now cold vinyl. How long had I been carrying the finger in my bag. And why out of all people was I supposed to throw it away. The summer road reeked of hot asphalt, the poppy-seed cake made me nauseous, as did the evening air, the reeds, the willows by the river. The water lapped against their roots and burbled, but still it wasn't deep enough. A few people out for a stroll, immersed in the evening, were walking toward me, their heads bowed. In the water flowing under this bridge and on to the next, the people walking alone turned into couples, the couples became foursomes. And there, along the railing of the bridge, where the suitcase filled with paper once stood, was the place for the finger. I didn't want to do it but that's where I went, I held the little package over the water and let it drop. The paper stayed wrapped and the package hit the water. The water rippled as it accepted the finger but refused to swallow it. The river would have preferred a whole person. For me even that one little piece was too much, and so was the fact that I didn't know whose it was. Nor whether the whole person was dead, or just his finger.

Albu never refers to the finger. Neither do I. Next day at ten sharp his sly forgetfulness is obvious. It was winking at me with every kiss of the hand. After the finger I no longer visit the bathroom at Albu's.

Nausea makes me soft, but sometimes it can be contagious, and when I want to infect others with my own revulsion, then I toughen up. The one person I told about the yellow-gray candy wrapper and its contents was Lilli. It was my first day back at the factory after three days with Albu. Nobody asked where I'd been. Nelu filled the time with furtive glances, by making coffee, airing the office and neatly stacking papers. I'd already made up my mind about the button samples he'd laid out on my desk that afternoon in a semicircle. But I couldn't say that the white ones were as beautiful as tooth enamel, the brown ones as open nutshells, the gray as raindrops in the dust.

After work I took Lilli to the café and got straight to the point. I skipped the outer shell and started right at the core. That's why Lilli twirled a strand of hair around her forefinger and backed her chair away from me. She thought I wouldn't notice, but a gap had opened up, I wasn't blind. Those mean slits of eyes were sharpened into daggers as she asked:

Are you sure it was a human finger.

That stubbornly cold tobacco flower was doing whatever it could to resist catching my nausea. I balled my hand into a fist and, holding it at the corner of the table, extended my index finger over the edge.

All right, what's this.

Take your finger away, she said.

Can it be mistaken for anything else.

I've seen it, take your finger away.

What was it you saw, a cigarette or a bird's foot.

Isn't it enough that I believe you, or do I have to say it.

Oh, so you believe me after all. I'm so lucky—how gracious of you.

I was gracious too, and since I didn't want to torment Lilli any longer, I retracted my finger and refrained from asking whether alley cats ate human fingers. Or how long it took a nail to blacken. Nor did I tell Lilli how afraid I was of the finger-hungry foxgloves in the garden, blooming on their long, slender stems. Or that, in the nausea of my poppy-seed cake, I had considered returning the package to Albu: that too was something I kept to myself. Or that while the package was floating in the river I found myself imagining how at ten sharp the next morning Albu would ask to have it back.

Last winter I bought myself a small jar of pickles at the grocer's next to the factory, Lilli said, and finished them in two sittings. The last ones I had to fish out with a fork, and when I pulled the fork out it was holding one pickle and one mouse. Isn't that more horrible than a finger.

But the mouse wound up in the pickles on its own, I said. And even if someone in the canning factory did put it in the jar on purpose, it wasn't meant for you. After all, anyone could have bought the pickles.

Anyone could have, but I was the one who did.

As if she was trying to defend Albu, Lilli ran her fingers through the hair at the back of her neck. Her hair was fluffed up behind her, and we sat facing each other in silence, our eyes refusing to meet. Out of nowhere, Lilli said:

I really have to pay my electric bill tomorrow.

Lilli and I had grown used to being together with silences that ran longer than the acceptable conversational lulls. And when one of us resumed talking, she would say whatever came into her head. When you know each other well enough, the mouse after the finger and the silence after the mouse and the electric bill after the silence are all one and the same thing. Then you go on talking, about something you never actually mention. And your forehead and mouth are as far apart as they can be.

There were two lines in front of the wooden cabins at the flea market; a young policeman was making sure nobody did his business outside, against the fence. The first toilet was missing a door and was unoccupied, but even so there were two lines. A man came out of the second carrying the door in his arms. He handed it to another man who'd been fidgeting outside the first toilet for some time; this man backed his way inside, putting the door up after him. Only then did the man who'd already been to the toilet button up his fly. His shoes were sprinkled.

Why don't you let him go first, a woman in sunglasses asked, he's still a little boy. A boy wearing shorts and sandals was lifting her dress and crying, she slapped him on the hands:

Leave my dress alone, stop it.

Let him cry, one man said, then he won't have to pee so often.

He took a matchbox out of his pocket and rattled it in front of the boy's face:

I'll let you have these.

The boy shook his head.

What's your name.

Zuckerfloh, the child said.

Your name isn't Zuckerfloh, the man said, that's not what they call you, and he rattled the matchbox. Then he said to the mother:

Don't worry, it's only sunflower seeds.

The woman took hold of the boy by the scruff of his neck:

Go on, tell him what your name is.

The child raised his arm to shield his face. Then it was too late, the water ran down his legs onto his sandals. I turned around and went back to Paul:

I can't get a door.

He had sold the last two aerials and was lounging on his bike. He tossed the bare string into the air.

What do you say to that.

Paul had stashed the money for my ring in his trouser pocket, where it was safe. He walked with me back to the cabins. There were still two lines. The door was a piece of sheet metal the size of a tabletop. Flies were buzzing, the people in lines were quarreling, you could see their gold-and-black molars, the worn-down stumps and gaps between the teeth. Paul pushed his way forward. Deals were struck:

You'll get my door. Then I'll get it. Then he will.

But as soon as the next person had relieved himself and carried out the door, whatever deals had been made were instantly forgotten. People were desperate, there was shouting. The policeman was leaning against the fence, munching cookies and cleaning one fingernail after the other with a red plastic comb.

Stop shouting, he ordered without looking up.

Why don't you help the people who need it, said a woman with a ponytail. I'm pregnant, I can't stand up any longer, my feet are ready to drop off.

Where are you pregnant, an old woman asked, giving the

policeman a look. Maybe in your ass, because you sure don't have much of a belly.

I'm not a referee, the policeman said.

The pregnant woman: Christ Almighty, it's easier to have twins than get hold of this door.

And it's better to have twins than two peg legs, the policeman laughed. I'll make sure you get the door before your feet really do break off.

He slipped the comb into his jacket, crammed a piece of cookie into his mouth, and stood in front of the occupied toilet.

That's right, pregnant or not, she gets the door next, she's been standing here for ages.

The pregnant woman promised Paul her door. When she came out of the toilet, she let go of the sheet metal before she could see who was tugging at it. The fat man who was supposed to be behind Paul waved his hands and swore, it was his door now. Paul never took his eyes off the toilet, and when the door started to wobble from inside, Paul grabbed hold of it and hoisted it away.

Hey, not while I'm at my devotions, not so fast, the fat man said, inside the shithouse you're communing with God, and outside you find that all hell's broken loose.

With God, said the policeman, or else just with some jackass who just went inside the shithouse and who happens to look exactly like you.

Paul shoved me into the cabin and positioned the sheet of metal in front. It turned out there was no roof, and heaven sent down its meddlesome green flies. Two filthy boards for standing on lay over a hole in the ground. It would have been easy to slip. I searched for two dry spots. Written on the wall in red paint was:

Life is really full of shit,
There's no choice but to piss on it.

I could hear the people outside, Paul was shouting too. In here it was safe. You can't become any less than the stuff that stinks beneath your feet. When the fat man spoke of God, did he mean that you could become drunk off the acrid fumes in here. I breathed deeply, I refused to hurry, and despite the risk of slipping, I shut my eyes. Not until I was back outside did I become a piece of human filth. I walked through the market next to Paul, the rows of people with their junk were beginning to scatter. Cigarette stubs lay strewn among the patterned imprints of molded rubber soles. The dust swirled up to our necks, I should have thanked Paul for helping with the door, but I couldn't get a word out. My gold ring was sold—six thousand lei was a fortune for me—and in all that filth. The dust was moving in the same direction as our feet, leading us on. The wind picked up in longish gusts and then dropped off. The wire fence that enclosed the market caught scraps of paper and old clothes. Paul folded his tarp smaller and smaller until it turned into a blue briefcase, which he wedged into one of the panniers on his motorcycle. Then Paul spat on his fingers and counted the money into my open palm, my elbow lost track and yielded to his touch. He finished counting out the banknotes, and I waited for his fingers to migrate from our business dealings to my pulse.

My beach ball and the brooch were still lying on the newspaper, not a single person had shown any interest, I wanted to walk away and leave them lying there. Paul blew up the beach ball and tossed it into the air. It flew away from me, like a huge scoop of watermelon breaking free from the ground and the dirty Sunday. It was so beautiful, now that it no longer belonged to me. And I, I wanted to hunker down and laugh with my eyes and cry with my mouth. It was the first moment of my ass-backward happiness with Paul. And right in the middle of it he asked:

What does a person do on a Sunday with full pockets and an empty heart?

He picked up the brooch and polished it on his trouser leg—a glass cat with a curved, copper-wire mustache. He fastened it to his shirt. As Paul pushed the motorbike along through the marketplace, the mustache twitched and the cat started to breathe.

If you like we can ride up to the old game preserve, he said, they have a restaurant in the park where you can sit outside.

Only if you throw the cat away, I said, you look like a vagrant.

I don't think so, he said, but still he tossed it away in the dust behind him, just missing a man who simply glanced up briefly as he hurried past with the long strides of someone who was running late.

His mother-in-law's waiting for him with chicken soup, said Paul, no need to hurry, by now it'll be cold anyway.

He had sold my wedding ring in this dust and wind, did he think I was some big-hearted floozy he could go out with and blow all that money. I knew the small botanical garden inside the former game preserve and I knew the Latin names for a few of the plants from walks I had taken there with my husband and his parents. Back then I was living at their place, downstairs in a room that opened onto the yard, so you could enter the room right from the garden path. In winter, instead of warmth, the coal-burning stove blew air as thick as incense up to the ceiling. From spring until late autumn, there were trails of ants along the walls and window frames, clusters of ants in the corners of rooms and drawers, and busy lone ants on the table and in the bed. Even in the kitchen. My mother-in-law doled out the soup. When her husband pushed his bowl over to be served, she would use the ladle to swirl the contents of the pot for a while, as if searching for chunks of vegetables. Actually she was stirring the ants to the sides. Despite her efforts some would still be floating in her husband's bowl. He would nudge them to the edge with his spoon and act as if the whole thing was completely out of the ordinary.

Where did these come from.

My mother-in-law said:

Don't get so excited. It's just pepper.

If that's just pepper, then I'm a nightingale.

It's ground pepper, my dear.

Since when does pepper have legs, he asked.

After the divorce, I had stuffed my clothes and things into two sacks and moved out. Since that day on the bridge I never used suitcases. My husband followed me to the gate with the stone from the Carpathians in a plastic bag. I nearly forgot it, and now I absolutely need it for cracking nuts. I felt ageless, for the most part I couldn't tell whether I was free or lonely. Being alone was neither a burden nor a pleasure. I didn't regret anything from my three years of marriage except that I had stayed two too many. I got my hair cut short, bought clothes. I also bought bedding for my newly rented flat, and started paying installments on a refrigerator and a couple of rugs. I wanted a change, and quickly, while this new phase was still fresh and leading me in a particular direction. Lilli never needed to change, she had no need of vanity; after all, what can happen to a cool tobacco flower. When love was over, she came out the other side looking great. Lilli knew all about squandered feelings, but she also knew that there'd soon be another pair of eyes hungering after her. I wanted to reshape myself with my own hands, but for that your hands need to be holding a wallet full of bills. I bought everything on impulse, without thinking. Compared to today, my worries were tiny, that was before I wrote the notes. I'd go through my paycheck in just two or three afternoons and then borrow money. Not only from Nelu, also from people I knew only slightly. The borrowed money ran through my fingers just as quickly, and went toward clothes. In the morning I'd come into the office and the first thing I'd do was place my handbag mirror on my desk. In between going over the lists of buttons I would constantly check my appearance. Every day Nelu praised me more. But you can't get a haircut every day, so to maintain my conviction that things weren't so bad, the only thing left was new clothes. For a day, at least, they were newer than my face. Of course I worried about my debts, but still I kept on buying. My eyes were wide and feverish, only my throat felt constricted. The spur of the moment was always more powerful than my guilty conscience. In the afternoon sun on the Korso, people turned to look at Lilli because she was beautiful and at me because I was walking arm in arm with her and singing loudly:

O the tree has its leaves,
the tea has its water,
money has its paper,
and my heart has snow that's fallen astray.

We acted as if we were drunk, I staggered and sang, Lilli staggered and laughed so hard she was crying. Until I said:

A dress doesn't run up debts, neither does a shoe. Neither do I. But money does. With some people, money grows back like whiskers on a chin, but my chin stays pretty smooth. Let's say there's a little money in my bag, then I can say I have something. Next thing you know it's in the cash register and suddenly I no longer have anything even though it's right there where I can see it, just a few inches away from my bag. The money's still worth the same amount, it's just that it's no longer mine, what do you make of that.

Once you're old it starts growing of its own accord, Lilli said, but is that a good reason to want to be old. Don't worry, none of the people you've borrowed from is going to lose sleep over a couple of bills. After all, you're not running away.

Lilli was mistaking the vanity I'd recently been unable to suppress with independence. After all, I wasn't going to run away. At least not from the factory, though perhaps from my common sense, that little iron doll in my head, like that rusty St. Anthony lying on the tablecloth at the end of New Year's Eve.

As long as I lived with my in-laws, whenever I stood in the garden I couldn't get over my stunned shock that the wild roses my father-in-law had hastily grafted would flower each summer in knotty buds of velvet. The new canes never reverted. Grafting roses seemed to me like having a face-lift on your hips. I put all sorts of flowers in the room, but never a grafted rose. Who could say it wouldn't go on changing after it had been cut. The leaves were the only thing I could change about myself after the separation, no matter how hard I tried. After the long married squabbles there were days when no one shouted at me. Every day brought me further away from other people, I had been placed out of the world's sight, as if in a cupboard, and I hoped it would stay that way. I developed a yearning for being alone, unkempt, untended—later, this disappeared and then showed up again in my mother. That's when I visited her for the last time and saw her stripped of all secrets, the only person left in the house, utterly alone. And I didn't feel any sympathy. In contrast to her, I did not postpone this yearning in myself. I'm not that tough, and above all I was younger than she: in her case, everyone close to her had died, and I had flown the nest. I could see myself in her as she resigned herself to the new circumstances—as if I were the mother and she the child. She would stand in the light of the window and seem like such a stranger it drove you crazy, she would stand by the dish rack in the kitchen and seem so familiar you wanted to run. And as she moved about the house she would alternate between one state and the other. But I realized that this craving for solitude was better suited to later life, and that it had affected me too young, too early.

I lived in a room rented from a skinny man who was always smiling. His smile seemed to be a facial feature rather than an expression. His shoulders were hunched, his collarbones rounded: it was like finding a birdcage at my door whenever he came for the rent. The skin on his face was transparent, as if his bones were rubbing it thin: no wrinkles, and yet very old. I made up some excuse for the fifth time and asked him in for a cup of tea. He declined, nodding and chirping, and I wondered how much longer this birdman would put up with me. Wouldn't he be angry if he got so worked up his skin wore through completely.

Leading a life of unkempt solitude was definitely not the right thing for me. But with Nelu I had stumbled into a real mess, I was trapped in his hatred. We had spent ten days on official business in a small town between the Danube and the Carpathians. He had been designated to make the trip and could choose someone to travel with him, he suggested me. The idea of going somewhere was fine as far as I was concerned. I hadn't imagined that Button Central, as the town was nicknamed in the factory, would be particularly attractive, but I certainly hadn't envisaged this wasteland consisting of ten rows of grimy prefab houses surrounded by concrete slabs and building sites overgrown with grass, where nothing was being built and nothing cleared away. Because it was home to the largest button factory in the country, the place was officially designated a town and not a village. A winding asphalt road ran for three kilometers through a field of nettles, from the hotel to the factory gates. In the wind the nettles rose and fell, a sea of blackish green you had to swim across. Early each morning we took that road, which was continuously losing itself and starting over. The nettles grew higher than our heads and even on the ninth day I could easily have lost my way. It wasn't the first time Nelu had been there, he was as familiar with the nettles as he was with the button factory. Our shoes were muddied by the mixture of dust and dew. At eight we wiped them with Nelu's handkerchief, outside the entrance, then made the rounds of the offices and departments with lists and swatches of cloth. By five in the afternoon I was half blind from looking at buttons made of plastic, mother-of-pearl, horn, or yarn, with two, three, or four holes, and buttons with stems wrapped in linen and velvet. Seen in these quantities, the buttons were like pills in a drug factory. Instead of being sent to the clothing factories to be sewn into clothes, they should have been packaged in boxes and sent out to the pharmacies, to be taken three times a day after meals. In the afternoons, the nettle road was just as blackish green as it was in the mornings. The dew had dried, the dust was white. Birds were squawking, who knows where they were hiding, there were none in the air. On the way back to the hotel we talked about seasonal buttons, prices, and delivery schedules.

From the front rooms of the hotel you could see the red,

single-story railway station. A white goat was grazing beside the tracks, tied to a stake. Inside the circle of its tether it was nibbling blue chicory and scorched grass. Or simply standing there looking down the tracks. The coming night swallowed ground, stake, and tether. Only the goat remained, a shimmering patch. High up on the gable shone the bright face of the station clock.

This was now the second night I had been lying in my bed, staring at the clock. The freight trains were rolling right across the sky, there was no chance of getting any sleep. From the first day on everything was all business and no pleasure—even the night, which was packed with trains. In between the trains there was a racket coming from the hall, men's voices speaking Russian. Already on the second night I had taken the heavy cut-glass vase and placed it beside my pillow, just in case. The tap water tasted of chlorine, and the chlorine tasted of the sleep I wasn't getting. I drank without thirst, only so as to have to get up and then lie down again. In the evenings we ate in the restaurant. Along the wall next to our round table was a long banquet table. I counted thirty-four people seated around it, small men with broad cheekbones, eyes and hair as black as night, wearing summer suits made of gray cloth and white collarless shirts.

They all sit together, the waiter said, so they can spend the evening talking about how to piss on horseback or sew buttons with a sickle. A delegation from Azerbaijan, they've already spent one week here in the button factory on an official exchange, on top of that they'll spend next week on a goodwill visit.

Where, I asked.

Also in the button factory, he said and winked. Mind you, the goodwill started on the very first day. Ever since they've been here, five girls from the button factory have been sneaking in after midnight to the back rooms on the ground floor. Outside the rooms it's all push and shove, and inside they're wailing away like bagpipes. The moment one of them's shot his bolt, the next climbs up on top. Just listening to all that sperm being sprayed around makes you crazy. This'll mean a litter of little ones in town, let me tell you, a whole nest of snotty, flat-nosed, half-Asiatics.

It was always the same man doing the talking at the long table, he spoke curtly and quickly as if he were berating the others, but without any sign of anger in his face. The rest would listen, occasionally all of them would laugh, including the one who had just been speaking harshly. The man frequently looked over at me. I allowed his eyes to meet mine since I had nothing better to do. Nelu went over the season's buttons one more time. I would gladly have said something about the Azerbaijanis, but no sooner had I remarked how many there were of them than Nelu informed me:

You shouldn't count people. They can sense you're doing it.

What if they do, why shouldn't you count them—after all, they're there. It would have been easier to talk about the fields of nettles or the station goat, but they didn't interest him as much as the Azerbaijanis. Nelu looked pretty well rested to me. So he can sleep despite the noise of the trains, I thought, he and the goat. A clockwork man who sleeps by night so he can do his job during the day—the perfect man for business trips. The whole point of this trip had been ridiculous from the start. Ordering buttons from a road of nettles that flooded your vision so that you lost sight of the mountains of clothes waiting at the factory. On the third night I started staring at the station clock at eleven, and was still staring at two on the dot. The trains would first whoosh in the distance like trees, then they sounded like iron in the sky, and finally they came crashing through your head loud enough to split it in two. A wounded silence followed, then dogs started barking until the next train came along. My brain slowly pieced itself back together. At one moment, when no train was passing, I heard somebody knocking at my door. I took the vase from beside my pillow and yelled:

Pashyol tovarish—I yelled in Russian for whoever was knocking to get lost.

It's me.

There in the doorway stood Nelu, in his pajamas, barefoot.

I've been knocking for some time.

I thought you were able to sleep. I can't sleep a wink here next to this station.

He sat on the bed with his head in his hands. I opened the window and saw the shimmering patch of the goat asleep in the dark, a red train signal just beyond the clock, and away in the distance a green one. Nelu lay down.

It's because of you that I can't sleep.

The window stayed open, we pulled the covers over us. I knew that our hungry groaning would be coming along soon, like the trains on the tracks. It was all right with me. Actually one day and one night in that wasteland was enough to bring me to the point where I would have opened the door for any one of the Azerbaijanis. I might have greeted him first with the vase, but in the end I would have let him in between my legs. Nelu panted, clutched at my breasts, we lay skin to skin near that railway station, and he talked of feelings, of love. I let him talk.

I let him talk because I thought I could straighten him out once we were back home. Maybe my feelings just needed more time.

Nelu came every evening around eleven. The ceiling light was off, the bulb above the sink was on. The curve of a neck merged with a shoulder, the lines of his angled arms and legs began to blur, two white eyes caught in the light, that was Nelu. All the rest was darkness. What that desolate town had worn down, love would now restore. He wanted me all night long, his flesh and brain were in complete agreement, they met at the place where thinking stops. But I got nothing out of it, I whimpered without ever forgetting where I was. I looked at the station clock and it gazed back. Inside my skull everything stayed as bright as that segmented dial on the gable. On my own I would never have taken that step to counter the desolation. And if I had, then it would have been with an Azerbaijani. He would have made the night speed by, one night or all the nights that were still to come. But in the restaurant, at the long table, I wouldn't have recognized him. Every evening at dinner I would have felt as if I was looking for one particular button among thirty-four identical ones. So a new one might just as well have come every night, for all they differed in appearance. At most the only way I might have been able to tell who it was would have been from the way he spoke, the way he moved. Or maybe they were all the same in bed, too. After the trip I would never again see the man I had spent ten nights with, or any of the ten men I had spent one night with. Nelu had started it, it wasn't my doing. About two o'clock every night I sent him back to his room. Even on the last night he was reluctant to go, but he was well-behaved and obedient, not wanting to spoil a good thing.

At five in the morning before we boarded the train for home, the goat was wandering around the stake. I gave it a piece of bread, which it gobbled up without first sniffing. The minute I was in the train compartment I fell asleep, catching up on all those nights, oblivious to the sound of the train's motion or anything else around me. When the train arrived at Central Station and Nelu woke me, my head was leaning against his shoulder, how had that happened. We walked through the noise of the city morning to the bus stop. Nelu was carrying his bag by his side, I carried mine between us to prevent him from putting his free arm around me. Outside the red station back at Button Central, as the goat was eating the bread in the cold morning air and Nelu was putting on his jacket, I knew no love lay in store for us.

The next few days at the office, before we went home, I said:

No, I'm not coming home with you. And no, you're not coming to my place.

Why, Nelu asked.

Whether ten days or three years, men were always demanding a reason. Nelu said it was impossible for there not to be one. After I separated from my husband, I wanted a life that went with my short hair. As long as I was still young, I wanted to go to the kind of beautiful country the clothes were exported to. I wanted to be worth clothes like that, and even prettier ones, and I wanted a generous husband to buy them for me. Three girls from the nursery gardens had married Italians. My father-in-law asked them about it and told us at home how it was done. Evidently there were men who craved the flesh of girls from these parts, usually bachelors, respected businessmen, who didn't get around to marrying until their mothers were in their graves. They were the kind of mild-mannered, persnickety gentlemen in whom you could hardly tell caring demeanor from approaching senility, well-groomed men getting on in years. Perhaps I would acquire Lilli's taste yet, if it meant getting out of this place. You didn't necessarily need to be a beauty, all you needed was the freshness of youth. And a modest manner. Marriages were allowed two years after you applied. Then you moved straight into the bosom of a family, straight from being bare-assed poor to having a marble vase on the table set with knives and forks—solid silver if you were lucky. I just wanted to kill the two years until I could go. It was all about Italy, it had nothing to do with him.

It's not because of you, I said. You're not the reason. Neither am I. We were just on a business trip.

His face froze up. Then his eyeballs glistened and turned into little squares. Out shot his arm, and he slapped me. He was better at that than he was at making coffee, tying shoelaces, or sharpening pencils. The blow was well aimed, and my head throbbed. I laughed, although my laughter faded. All right, maybe there was some justice in knocking my head against the doorframe. But it was unjust of him to report me one week later for those notes addressed to Italy. And to go one step further with the notes for Sweden, which he wrote himself and put in trouser pockets so that I got fired. That was persecution. And as for the notes for France . . .

We're there, Grandma, says the driver. Now all the old lady has to do is stand up and in ten or fifteen shakes of her head she'll be at the door. From the back of the car comes a clanking of pails and a shuffling of shoes. I'd be happy to get out here and buy myself something, maybe a single apple, you don't have to stand in line for that. If I were quick about it I wouldn't even miss the tram. It's almost nine o'clock, but not ten sharp, not yet. A grass-green summer apple, even if the early ones do tend to be wormy and covered with splotches like birthmarks.

When you bite into them the juice spurts out and your mouth puckers up. An apple like that would suit the blouse that grows. I could eat it on the tram or right after I got off, just before ten. Or I could save it for later. I could put it in my pocket so Albu wouldn't see it. If Albu keeps me there I won't be getting anything to eat for a long time. But what if the apple cancels out the nut and somehow causes Albu to do exactly that. I could imagine the toothbrush and toothpaste might infect the apple. Then no matter how hungry I was I wouldn't be able to stomach the apple. The man with the brief-case jumps up from his seat and walks up to the driver: I'm just going to buy myself some aspirin, you'll be here a little while, won't you. Not very long, says the driver, I wouldn't mind a few tomatoes, but we're running late. If you wait, I'll bring you some, says the man with the briefcase. The driver opens his bottle: No, I'll make up time on the next go-round, then I'll be able to get them myself. Before drinking he wipes the top of the bottle with his hand, as if the last person to drink from it had been someone other than him.

My head was spinning that Sunday after the flea market when I sat behind Paul on a motorcycle for the first time in my life. The streets were arching upwards. In the city center large families were leaving the church in scattered clusters that lingered outside the door. After all the singing and praying the adults had much to discuss, while the children were once again free to fidget and laugh. An old lady wearing black with white stockings was walking down the lane lined with sycamores as if she were passing through a valley. She was calling out:

Georgiana.

But nobody was answering. A few trees farther down,

though, I saw a girl standing next to a large trash bin. She was wearing a red ribbon in her hair and was singing a song. The old lady seemed at a loss, caught between the adults who were walking at a pace set by their chatting, and the child who didn't come when she was called. I turned to look back as we rode past until I ran out of neck to twist. The black clothes disappeared, and I felt the thrumming of the motorbike in every finger.

My father went to church every Sunday his whole life long. If Mama or Grandfather or I didn't go with him, he went by himself. On his way home, Papa would stop at the bar behind the park and treat himself to a brandy and a foreign cigarette. By one o'clock on the dot he'd be sitting at the table ready for Sunday dinner. He kept going to church even in the last years of his life, when his very bones were rotten with sin. In his place I would have stayed at home, if I had that much sin to account for. I can't believe that on Sunday he'd promise God he'd finish with the woman with the braid—given that he'd already arranged to meet her the very next day. I'd seen it: on Mondays the woman came to the market without her child. She had spent Sunday with her husband, just as my father did with his wife, counting the hours. But by Monday evening neither God Almighty nor the devil himself could keep them apart. For Sunday dinner we had two chickens, whatever was left over we saved for supper. My father ate the combs from both chickens because he needed them for his Monday sin. And I shared the brain with Grandfather, so that I'd learn to hold my tongue like him. It's possible that Papa prayed to God for indulgence, since the Lord had to know there wasn't much going on with Mama. Jesus was hanging just to the right of the church door, high enough for the grown-ups to kiss his feet as they came in and out of the church. Children were lifted by their hips. For as long as it was necessary, my mother or my grandfather held me up, but never my father. Jesus had lost his toes, they'd been completely kissed away. When I was little my father said to me:

These kisses don't go away. They light up around your mouth when you die, on Judgment Day. Then it's easy to see who you are and you can enter Paradise.

What color do they light up, I asked.

Yellow.

And the kisses we give each other.

They don't light up, because they go away, he said.

Everyone who lived near St. Theodore's church was carrying a little dust from Jesus' toes on their lips. When I wanted to take the place of the woman with the braid, and my father clove to her flesh, I hoped her kisses wouldn't go away. That on Judgment Day they would light up darkly among all the glowing toe-kisses and give away the deceiver.

Lilli once said her mother no longer went to church because nowadays the masses all began with an intercession for the Head of State.

That's all well and good, I said, but she puts up with her husband taking his old bones to his weekly meeting next to the newsstand.

She puts up with it, said Lilli, because she has to.

My head was still flooded with the ride, even though Paul and I had been sitting for some time at the park. On the last stretch where the road ran through the forest the lower branches snatched at our hair. The trees were humming with green, the whole sky was made of leaves. I had scrunched up my neck and implored him:

Not so fast.

Paul brought his chair up close to mine and kissed me with his mouth ringed with beer froth. I was dazed from the ride and now this kiss on top of that. My heart was swinging back and forth by the thinnest of threads. I wanted to keep a clear head, but happiness didn't give me enough time. Much too slowly I began to grasp that happiness can be found even at a flea market—no matter that the place was filthy and full of junk and people from whom all I wanted was their money. That happiness doesn't need time so much as luck. One moment my fingers were cradling Paul's warm chin, the next they were clasping the cold neck of the beer bottle. Since we knew so little about each other we talked a lot, although mostly not about ourselves. Paul downed six whole bottles and was able to put away even more later that afternoon as families started coming into the woods. After eating Sunday dinner in their apartment blocks they wanted to hold on to the sky for just a little while longer, before the next week of confinement in the factories. An elderly couple took the two free seats at our table. Their wedding rings were thick and engraved with floral patterns, after the current fashion.

I'm asking you for the last time, said the woman.

I don't know, said the man.

Who does, then.

Not me.

What do you mean you don't. Don't pretend to be dumber than you are.

Don't spit when you're talking. I've forgotten, for God's sake.

What you've forgotten is your mind. You forgot that the day you were born.

That's for sure, otherwise I wouldn't have hooked up with your little birdbrain.

No, you'd still be in a mud hut with your mother.

You're a fine one to talk, sweetie.

Don't you sweetie me. Nobody else would put up with you.

Heavens, next thing you'll start crying for me.

What were you thinking just now.

What do you want me to say.

You must've been thinking of something.

No, I wasn't thinking of anything.

I don't believe you.

It's true.

You lie every time you open your mouth.

That's right, even when I'm fucking you.

That goes without saying.

All the same, you seem to want me often enough.

Because that's all you're good for.

Listen to you, you're nothing but a hole with a perm.

So tell me what happened, or keep quiet.

Stop it, I don't know.

Then who does . . .

After that it started all over again, round and round like a whirlpool, the tone became sharper, the mud hut became a chicken coop and the hole with a perm became a mattress with fringe. Their eyes shot poison at each other. The woman interrogated him as if they were the only two people there, while the man stared off into space as if he were all alone. The sun was still milky-white, you could hear the tall trees rustling, the sky was bearing down so low there was barely room for it among all the foliage, shoes were crunching through the gravel. He was clearly sick of her and at the same time completely dependent on her. And she never let any of us out of her sight. Even Paul and I were trapped, we said nothing, we refrained from looking at each other so she wouldn't think we were exchanging signals. Cut off from each other like that, listening and at the same time acting as if we were deaf, we couldn't imagine what she expected of him. Paul took his hand off the table, the woman noted the movement, glanced at me and waited to see what I would do. I leaned in Paul's direction, and he put his hand on my knee and said:

Come on.

I sat up straight. The woman was waiting for Paul's hand to reappear on the table. Paul must have sensed that and left his hand on my knee. With the other he beckoned the waiter over.

This is on me, for selling the wedding ring—may it have a happy future, I said.

I wanted to downplay my happiness. By chance the other two were quiet just then, they were listening to us the way Paul and I had listened to them. I was glad that they too were hearing something they didn't understand. Paul took some money out of his pocket, he wouldn't touch any of mine. The woman looked at her wedding ring, and Paul and I said in unison:

Goodbye.

We sounded like two wind-up talking dolls. The woman waved in reply, barely lifting her hand off the table. The man looked as if he needed us as allies and said:

All the best.

In his position he seemed more in need of luck than we were. We rode back through the trees to the leaning tower. That night was the first I spent at Paul's, and from then on I stayed.

We made love that first night until our bodies felt both older and younger, panting to the point of bursting and sighing calmly. Afterwards I heard barking, as if stray dogs were roaming the heavens. Then the street slumbered on to the ticking of the clock and everything below was silent. A gray dawn broke, still no light on the clock dial. Soon the trucks began making deliveries to the shops in the street. I got up and sneaked out of the room, carrying my clothes. I felt goose bumps as I stood in the hall, pulling my clothes over skin that was still warm from the bed. I wanted to put my shoes on quickly and leave before Paul woke up. But I didn't. Stay here just like the shoes, just like the cupboard hanging on the wall in the kitchen, and the sharp, bright swath of sunlight that's growing by the minute and crawling up the back of the chair onto the table. Stay here because all the papers being drafted, stamped, and signed, inside the factory dictate that every Saturday is followed by a Monday. I poured myself a glass of water and drank the mealy taste of my tongue. But I was not going to stay here like some bargain picked up at the flea market, in that case it would better to get up and get out. If you leave you can always come back. A red enameled tin can was standing on the table, I opened it, smelled the ground coffee, closed the lid, put the can back down and saw my greasy fingerprints, as well as what I had dreamed during the night:

My father was lying on a wooden table in the yard at home, he was wearing a white Sunday shirt, next to his left ear was a peach from one of the trees he had planted years before. A barrel-chested man with a birdlike face who in the dream was not my landlord was cutting out a square between the tips of my father's collar and his stomach, he was cutting through my father's shirt, from the third to the fifth button, very precisely as though the man had measured my father's chest with a ruler. He lifted a small whitewashed door of flesh.

I said: He's starting to bleed.

The man said: That's from his wife's melon. You see, she's crippled, she can't grow anymore and isn't any bigger than an egg. We're taking her out and putting in a peach.

He removed the melon from Papa's chest and replaced it with the peach. The peach was ripe, with red cheeks, but you could tell from the fuzzy hair it hadn't been washed.

It belongs to the woman with the braid, I said, it will never grow, she doesn't keep it fresh.

You've got to admit if there's one thing she knows about it's vegetables.

A peach is a fruit, I said.

We'll see, he said.

The man put the small door back on Papa's chest, it fit perfectly. He walked to the wall of the house, turned on the faucet and washed his hands with the garden hose.

Isn't the small door going to be stitched in, I asked.

No, he said.

What if it falls out.

The seal's airtight, it will heal over, I've done this before, he said; after all, I am a professional cabinetmaker.

After Paul and I had made love past all the waves of weariness, he fell into a peaceful slumber, while I fell into a sleep that was brimming with images. The small door of flesh might have come from the removable toilet door, the surgeon-landlord may have appeared since I now had money to pay what I owed. My father and the woman with the braid had no business here, and my wish to take her place had no right to show up on my first night with Paul.

The red coffee can was sparkling too much, the sun was making it giddy, the tin must be the one that's daydreaming instead of me.

Paul sneaked up behind me and clapped his hands over my eyes.

I've been thinking, you should move in with me.

I hadn't heard him coming and felt as if I'd been caught with my father.

No, I said.

But inside I had accepted, as if I had no choice. When he

uncovered my eyes, a woman was shaking out two white pillows in the window across the way, and I said:

Yes.

I had my doubts. And the very next moment I took four heaping spoonfuls of coffee from the tin and put them in the pot, and Paul said:

Good.

It was a beautiful word to say, because it couldn't be bad. Paul put a jar of apricot marmalade on the table and cut far too many slices of bread.

In the mornings I usually grab something to eat as I'm heading out the door, so that I can get something in my stomach without actually sitting down to a real breakfast. But this time I remained seated. I told him about my father and the small door of skin, and about the melon and the peach. I left out the woman with the braid. Nor did I mention the fact that the red coffee tin reflected the dream. Nor that I was wary of the tin just as I would be of a stranger. With people to whom I take an immediate dislike, the wariness soon wears off unless I talk about it, that's how it was with Nelu when I started work at the factory. But the reason I'm shy of objects is because I like them. I transfer the thoughts that are against me onto them. Then these thoughts go away, unless I talk about them—just like my wariness of people. Maybe it all collects in your hair.

After I separated from my husband, in the quiet days when no one was shouting at me anymore, I started noticing other people's wariness of strangers. I saw how they combed their hair in public. In the factory, in the city, in the streets, and trams, buses, and trains, while waiting in front of a counter or standing in a line for milk and bread. People comb their hair at the movies before the light goes out, and even in the cemetery. While they're parting their hair you can see their wariness of others collecting in their combs. But they can't comb it out completely if they go on talking about it. The fear of strangers sticks to the comb and makes it greasy. People who talk about it can't get rid of their fear of strangers; their combs are always clean. I thought back: Mama, Papa, Grandfather, my father-in-law, my husband—all had filthy combs, Nelu too, and Albu. Lilli and I sometimes had clean ones and sometimes they were sticky. That's right, that's exactly how it was with our fear of strangers, our talking and our keeping quiet.

Paul and I were drinking coffee, the sun was sprawled across the table. I had told him my dream and nothing more, nothing at all about the combs. Paul was wary of my dream, he avoided my gaze and stared out the window.

Weak nerves, he said. At any rate, your surgeon promised the door would heal over.

Out beyond the glass in the window three swallows flew across a patch of sky. Either they were flying an advance party or they were a separate unit and had nothing to do with the countless birds that followed. I should never have started counting but already I was moving my lips.

Are you wondering how many there are, Paul asked.

I do a lot of counting. Cigarette butts, trees, fence slats, clouds, or the number of paving stones between one phone pole and the next, the windows along the way to the bus stop in the morning, the pedestrians I see from the bus between one stop and the next, red ties on an afternoon in the city. How many steps from the office to the factory gate. I count to keep the world in order, I said.

Paul fetched a picture from the other room, it hadn't been on the wall, otherwise I would have seen it. Still, it was framed, and a cockroach lay pressed under the glass.

When my father died I had the photo framed and hung it in the room. After only two days the cockroach showed up and joined the family. The cockroach is right, when somebody dies you start acting out of fear for yourself, as if you'd loved the deceased more than the living. Then I took it down.

In addition to the cockroach I saw Paul's mother, with dimples in her cheeks, one arm placed on the left hip of her summer dress, the other around her husband's hip. Paul's father was wearing a peaked cap, a checked shirt with the sleeves rolled up, wide knee-length shorts, long calf-length socks, and sandals. He had curled one arm around his wife's shoulder, the other was on his right hip. They were both the same height, pressed against each other, their arms on their hips like two handles. At that point I wasn't yet thinking about plums leaning cheek to cheek. In front of the proud parents stood a stroller—one of the first models with a shade you could roll up and down. Here it was rolled up, and inside the stroller sat Paul, the starched brim of his bonnet arching across his forehead like a crescent moon, a bow dangling beneath his chin, all the way down to his stomach. His left ear was poking out of the bonnet. One tiny hand was holding up a toy shovel. A blanket had been kicked almost completely out of the stroller. In the distance you could see a hill, plum trees in white blossom, and, at the top of the picture, the metal works, blurry like the smoke from its chimneys. A family of workers in a happy world of industry, a picture fit for the paper. Then, sitting at the table in the sunshine, I had to tell Paul about my perfumed father-in-law on the white horse, a picture also from the fifties.

Your father is nothing like the man on the white horse, I said, but both of them are Communists. One at the blast furnace in the city, the other traipsing through village streets in shiny riding boots. One slaving away in the service of glowing steel, raising its worth above all reason, the other riding people down, hounding them into a corner and reeking of perfume.

At my wedding my grandfather danced only one waltz with me. He pressed his mouth to my ear and said: Back in 1951 that bastard already stank of perfume, and now he's joining the family. Wants to have his fun with us again, does he. Wants to eat here with us, does he. Fine, he can have a plate at his seat of honor. I have a little something for him back at home, a little poison for his food. He said the words so calmly, keeping time to the waltz and breathing lightly—for all the world a man who kept his promises. My long dress swayed and billowed, but inside I was as stiff as a fence-post. Grandfather stepped on my hem a few times and apologized. I only said:

It doesn't matter.

Though it mattered a lot that I was sick of that long dress. I wished he would step on it until I was no longer inside it. After the dance he led me back to my seat beside my husband at the head of the table. Three chairs down, my father-in-law was bending over his daughter's shoulder, her earring had come unfastened. My grandfather stroked my sleeve.

And you intend to stay with him.

I had no chance to ask whether he meant my father-in-law or my husband. He walked off through the hall, he meant both. I searched for him with my eyes. My husband tugged at my hand so that my eyes would turn back to him. And when they did, and when my fingers were nestled between his hands and resting on his black trousers, I wanted him to go on holding me forever and live with me as if he had three hands. Whatever was gnawing at my grandfather was no fault of ours. Then the music started up again, the meal was served. The waiters ran with the dishes between the tables, coming in at the door through which my grandfather had left and not returned, not even for the banquet.

My father-in-law had eaten, his hands were shiny with grease, his fingernails looked varnished, his cheeks hot, not a trace of poison in his weasel-like eyes. His plate was littered with the chicken bones he had sucked clean. The band started playing again. The chef appeared wearing a white apron, a blue kerchief, and a white cap like a sailor's, and carried the wedding cake to the bridal table. It was in the form of a filigreed house, three stories with windows and curtains made of icing and two wax doves on the roof. The chef handed me the knife, it was my job to slice up the house, cutting through the thick white crusts into the brown walls, until each plate had a piece. My father-in-law's soup bowl and his plate from the main course had been cleared away with all the rest. He held out his dessert plate:

Only a thin slice, please.

But his thumb and index finger were asking for a big piece. Suddenly my hearing failed me and I couldn't breathe; just as if my food had been poisoned, my heart began to feel furry. I went in search of my grandfather. He wasn't outside, he wasn't in the kitchen, or hiding with the instruments in the musicians' storeroom. He was sitting by the barrels of wine and brandy, waiting for nothing and nobody, and when I started to sit down beside him, he said:

You'll get your dress dirty here.

I leaned against the fire escape in the corner.

He was sprinkling himself with perfume while we were herded to the station. We rode for two weeks in the train before we stopped—some four hundred and fifty families dumped out in front of a wooden marker set in the middle of nowhere. Rows of stakes in dead straight lines, sky above, clay below, with nothing between but the damned crazy thistles and us. The sun scorched everything in sight. For several days your grandmother and I did nothing but dig ourselves a hole in the ground in front of our stake and cover it with thistles. They tore your skin when you picked them. The wind from the east was searing, and then the thirst, no water for three kilometers. We set out for the river with pots and bowls, but by the time we got back to our hole in the ground all the water had spilled out. We had scabies and lice, your grandmother had to have her head shaved, I did too. Only it's different for women, even thistles have that bit of white down—it was flying around everywhere, the wind never let up. Your grandmother said: See, there's the white horse, it's following us, next we'll be growing hooves and a hide. She lashed out at something only she could see and hunched her shoulders and shouted: Get away, there. She started wandering, even the longest days weren't long enough for her to find her way back through all the holes in the earth. I'd call out: Anastasia, Anastasia. You could hear her name bouncing off every thistle leaf, but she didn't answer. The shouting made the thirst unbearable. When I did find her she'd be eating muddy clay as if she were lapping up water. Often she'd laugh with her brown, broken teeth, first her gums were cracked, then they shriveled up, and then they disappeared so that there was nothing left to bleed. Eyes like an owl's, and that grinding in her mouth, a ghost squatting in the mud. I was about to die of thirst, and she wasn't embarrassed in the least, she just clawed at the earth and swallowed it. I slapped her hands, hit her across the mouth. She was so afraid of the thistledown, she'd plucked out her lashes and eyebrows. Her eyes were as naked as her head, two drops of water. Dear God, I was so thirsty I wanted to drink them. I made it my task to keep her from dying, to keep her there with whatever strength I had, because love was out of the question. I struck her harder and harder, because she didn't know her own name, how old she was, where she came from or who she was with. We were both one step away from death, she was mercilessly mad and good, and I was too goddamned clearheaded and bad. She had taken leave of herself and left me to the world: Death was calling Anastasia even louder than I was. That great deceiver, and she was under his spell. But you can't just take things as they come. I had to hit her, many people looked on, and nobody intervened. Other people weren't any better than I was, but what does that concern me. I was rough, and she never stopped being good, that's all. I wasn't right in the head. I gloated as I shoved her by the back of her neck and yelled: No one's turning into a horse around here, we're going to dry out like two bean pods, just wait and see. There aren't enough trees around to make a single coffin—you'll have to be mine and I'll be yours. Sometimes she'd shuffle along and squeeze her eyes shut, other times she'd droop and stare at me and ask: Are you a guard, do you get paid. Thank God she didn't realize the scoundrel who was talking like that was her own husband. No sooner was she in her grave than the first winter arrived. She had it good, she didn't see the next wave of white down, the blizzards that came lashing across the steppe worse than any snow that ever covered the earth. It never settled, it was always moving. Whetted sharp by the sun, it came in waves and waves of little knives. And in the summer the clay started to run because of the heat, yellow and yellow-red and gray. Sometimes bluish white, as if you'd swum to the end of the sky, then you felt even dizzier than you already were. Snow burns in a different way than clay, even if you turn your back to it, it sucks the water out of your eyes. Many of us lost our wits, one at a time or in couples, it didn't matter anymore. Shortly after she died a tractor came to fill in our foxholes.

We had to put up buildings—after all, we were human beings, they said. We could forget about returning home. Perhaps it was better like that, I had to tread a lot of clay, and dry the bricks, the weather was wet, winter was coming. I had no time for thoughts. I bartered her moldy clothes for seven planks. Like everybody else I built a house, can you imagine, it had to be eight meters by four meters and contain 2,300 bricks. Every brick thirty-eight centimeters long, twenty wide, and twelve thick. And every wall as thick as the brick was long, though in that weather everything turned out crooked and warped. And for the roof there was straw, thistles, grass, but the wind kept blowing it all away. You had to paint a marker outside on the wall—a square, zigzags, a circle—in place of a house number, because numbers weren't allowed. To master death I painted a horse. I knew right up to the end that none of us would turn into a horse. But every winter the snow turned the whole place into one gigantic white horse. I held on in that house for four years, don't ask me how. Now you should go, said my grandfather, if you love his son, you should go.

Was it his fault, I asked.

He looked up.

You're asking the wrong question.

Was it my fault, I asked.

Is there anything he can do about it, said my grandfather. No, there isn't.

When I went back into the hall I felt I needed someone to help me crawl out of my skin. But nobody did, so I just wolfed something down. The wedding cake still had two windows left in half a wall, I ate a curtain. My husband was dancing with his mother and her white patent leather bag that dangled down his back. My father was dancing with my mother's white French twist. My father-in-law was dancing with his daughter and her

176

white shoes. I looked down at myself and saw that white was taking over my family. Who could do anything about it. Someone should be able to.

A horse is coming into camp
with a window in its head.
Do you see the tower looming high and blue . . .

my grandfather would sometimes sing as he worked in the garden. It was not a wedding song.

The tram has stopped at the signal pole. Another red light, says the driver. Who's it for, anyway. Nobody sets foot in the street for days on end, but they go and put in traffic lights and sit in their offices on their big fat asses. None of them bothers to come into town to look at their lights. They even get bonuses for having them installed, and I lose mine because I can't make the route on time.

The people standing in the car watch the light but don't say anything. One of them sneezes. Once, twice, three times. Traffic lights don't make you sneeze—it's the sun, that's what's set him off, four times, five. I can't stand it when someone sneezes so many times, it's always these small, scrawny men who can't stop and don't have any manners. With clods like these you're lucky if they cover their mouth the first time; after that you can forget it. You hope each sneeze is the last one, but then you can't help waiting for the next. Your brain gets addled, you start counting the sneezes, and that only encourages them. Now this guy's sneezing for the sixth time, why doesn't he hold his nose and take seven quick breaths, or hold his breath and count to sixty, then it'll all be over. He apparently doesn't know that trick, but I can't exactly tell him how by shouting from one end of the car to the other. Actually, holding your breath doesn't work for sneezing, that's for hiccups. He ought to rub his nose until it doesn't tickle anymore, that's the cure for sneezing. His eyes are as big as chestnuts, they'll pop out if he doesn't stop. But what do I care. His neck is bulging and turning red, his ears are burning. Here's number seven, *atchoo,* my head's spinning just from watching him . . . and why can't he make some other sound than *atchoo.* Finally he's stopped. No, here comes number eight. There won't be anything left of him, he'll sneeze himself away until all that remains is a ball of snot.

Paul placed the photo in the drawer and asked:

What did your father-in-law do back in the fifties.

He was a Party operative, I said, in charge of expropriation. My grandfather owned some vineyards on the hills in the neighboring village. The Perfumed Commissar confiscated my grandfather's gold coins and jewelry and placed him and my grandmother on the list for deportation to the Baragan Steppe. When my grandfather came back, his house belonged to the state. He had to go to court several times until they let him move back in, the bread factory had converted the rooms into offices. There was always a lot of talk about the house, mostly over dinner, but very little about my grandmother, things like:

She decided to die quickly, she didn't live past that horrible first summer. She couldn't wait, so she didn't live to see the mud hut.

The Perfumed Commissar didn't go back to that town until my wedding. And that was a rash thing to do, as it turned out. He probably thought no one would remember him, or maybe he just didn't think at all. After all, to him the deportees were

178

nothing more than a nuisance. He might have remembered some of the people who'd worked for him. But the rest of the rabble he only knew from the lists and not by their faces. For him my grandmother was simply a name; he selected her and then she died, just like many others. When he came back it was to celebrate the wedding. My grandfather recognized him immediately from his walk and from his voice—despite the new name. The name he'd used in the fifties was for official purposes, later he went back to his real name. The commissar's father had been a coachman who made his living with a cart and two bay horses. He delivered wood and coal as well as lime and cement. On occasion he also delivered coffins to the cemetery, if people couldn't afford the elegantly carved hearse. He swept up more horse manure in one day than he saw money in his lifetime. Whenever the cart was fully loaded, his sons had to run along behind him, to spare the horses, and when the cart stopped they had to unload or shovel or carry sacks. That white horse was a sign that my father-in-law had left the world of draft horses behind, he climbed out of the muck straight onto its back. Looking extremely out of place, he used to ride through the village, hating anyone richer than a carter. The perfume became his second skin. A perfumed Communist, who ever heard of such a thing, I asked Paul. What's a Communist, anyway.

Me, said Paul. I was well brought up, I did my homework like a good boy, and one day my father called me into the kitchen. His shaving bowl was on the table, and there was hot water on the stove. He lathered up my face until the soap got in my nostrils and then he fetched his razor. I could have counted all the whiskers on my face with one hand. But I was proud of myself, I started shaving and I joined the Party; as far as my father was concerned the two things went together. He explained that he had been born before his time and had no choice but to go along with whatever came. First he was a fascist; later he said he'd been in the Communist underground. As for me, he said, I was born when I was born and I had to stay ahead of my time. The few who really were Communists back then are right when they say: There used to be so few of us, but many are left. They needed these many, who hatched out of their old lives like wasps. Anyone poor enough became a Communist. So did many rich people who didn't want to end up in a camp. Now my father's dead, and if there's a heaven up there, you can be sure he's claiming to be a Christian. The motorcycle belonged to him. My mother was a machine fitter. Now she's retired and every Wednesday she meets her wrinkly old brigade in the café next to the hardware store in the marketplace. When I was little I used to walk through town with my father and he showed me his picture as a Hero of Labor on the plaque of honor in the People's Park. I preferred to look at the squirrels. The squirrels were all named Mariana and had to shell pumpkin seeds because people didn't have any nuts to feed them. You could buy pumpkin seeds at the entrance to the park. That's extortion, said my father, one whole leu for a handful of pumpkin seeds. He didn't buy me any.

Squirrels know how to feed themselves, he said.

I had to call Mariana with empty hands, and the squirrels came in vain. As I called I kept my hands in my trouser pockets. At the plaque of honor by the main pathway, my father said:

Don't look left and don't look right, son, just keep your eyes fixed straight ahead but remember to stay flexible.

Then he gave my cap a tug to one side so it slanted across my left ear, leaving my right uncovered, and we went on our way. At the crossroads he blinked and said:

First look left and then look right, son, to see if a car's coming. That's important when you're crossing a street but it's a dangerous way to think.

He only visited me once here in the city. He was proud of my living in a high-rise, it was so different from our house, with the mountain looming right in front of your nose, up here you have air and a view. He went out onto the balcony, but he never got a chance to appreciate the view. He stumbled on my tools and the aerials and asked:

What's this. You're selling things on the black market.

When he realized the aerials were designed to pick up foreign stations, he started talking about me as if I were some other person:

So my son has a taste for money. That's making a mockery of socialism. And what will come next. Sheer unadulterated capitalism. He can make aerials till he's blue in the face but he'll never belong to the people who flaunt their money hand over fist.

I said: It's not mocking anything to earn money, and it's not against the law.

To which he said: It's not exactly legal, either, but you didn't worry about that, did you.

And what do you mean by capitalism, I said. I'm not earning dollars, and besides, the Yugoslavs and Hungarians have socialism just like we do, even on television.

Lately the Party's had more profiteers than fighters, he said, and generally speaking, money ruins character.

But it's your own son you're talking about, and I'm the only one you've got. Besides, what have you achieved except a career melting iron for tractors and pitchforks for shoveling manure. We still don't have heaven on earth. But your brain is in full red bloom. When you stand before the Lord God Almighty, he'll see that glow on your forehead and ask: Well, little sinner, what have you brought me. Two corroded lungs, some herniated discs, chronic conjunctivitis, poor hearing, and a shabby suit, you'll say. And what have you left behind on earth. And you'll say: My Party book, a peaked cap, and a motorcycle.

My father just laughed: Hah hah hah, that's only if you wind up playing God. But, you know, even in heaven I'd be ashamed of you, since we'd have a bird's-eye view of all those rooftops with your black-market antennas.

I didn't want to go on, but he wasn't through. He looked at the clock and said: Hopefully there aren't many people in the city who think they need those foreign TV stations. Once they get their aerials, that'll be it.

I said: You're a mean old man, and you're jealous, even of me.

My father was out of breath and didn't respond, he pulled his cap down over his left ear, so that it looked exactly as it had on me as a child at the plaque of honor. Only now he was doing it to himself. He looked at the clock and said: No point to any of this, I'm hungry.

Your father was bitter, I said, else he wouldn't have been so pig-headed, but he wasn't a danger to others. My father-in-law clawed his way up the ladder. He'll never tell a living soul why he fell from grace, there are only rumors. But everybody remembers exactly how the Perfumed Commissar rode from house to house, tying his white horse in the shade of the trees and how he wrapped his whip around the horse's mane. And that the horse was called Nonjus. My grandfather said the farmers were made to bring hay and buckets of fresh water. The white horse ate and drank, while its rider searched the houses for grain and gold. He had papers with the field plots carefully mapped and numbered. After each expropriation he'd go back to his horse and unwrap the colorful woven leather whipcord. There was a silken tassel at the end of the cord and the base of the haft had a screw-on cap made of horn. He'd open this to get his pen. Then he'd take a sheet of paper out of his jacket and cross off a number. Whenever he rode through the village, the dogs would chase after him, barking. They sensed that the man on the horse was putting an end to the peaceful ways of the village. He hated those mutts, he'd crack his whip and that would goad them even more. They were little creatures, like barking cats, but they would race like the wind alongside the horse's hooves. Sometimes it took three, four, or even ten tries, but eventually the whip would catch them on the neck or between the ears. People would wait until late afternoon to remove the dogs from the street, when they knew he was finished riding for the day. The mutts lay stretched out stone dead, with their light-colored stomachs swelling up in the sun and their eyes and snouts covered in flies. First he rounded up the farmers with large holdings and turned them over to the security services, after that he went after the medium-sized farmers, then he moved on to the smallholders. He was a hard worker, after a while he was rounding up too many farmers, and ones who were too poor at that, so the gentlemen in the city sent whole groups of them back to the village on the next train.

One morning the white horse lay dead in the stable after eating poisoned bran. Day and night, local men were interrogated and beaten in the parish hall by two village ruffians who spelled each other in shifts. Three men were accused and arrested. All three are dead now, but none of them did it. One night the two thugs loaded the horse onto a trailer and hauled it off to be buried in the valley between the village and the town on the other side of the vineyards. My father-in-law accompanied them. He and one of the thugs sat on the trailer with a hurricane lamp perched next to the horse's carcass. They had to drink brandy because the horse stank so much. The other thug was at the steering wheel, sober. They drove up into the hills. It had been raining heavily, the tractor got bogged down in the soft earth. The next day the driver told how the crickets, frogs, and other night creatures in the soggy grass were screaming like mad throughout the night, and the horse's carcass stank to high heaven. The devil had us bagged up good and proper, he said. During the night, the great Communist started to rave. He stomped off aimlessly into the mud, sobbing and cursing. He kept throwing up, his eyes were practically popping out of his head, there was absolutely nothing left ⌜in his stomach. When the grave had been dug and the horse had been unloaded from the tractor rig, he threw himself to the ground and flung his arms around the horse's neck and refused ⌊to let go. The two thugs had to drag him into the driver's cab and tie him to the seat. And there he sat as they drove back, tied up, filthy, covered in vomit, and completely silent. When the tractor was halfway home and they were again on top of a hill, the driver untied him and asked: How about a short break. He shook his head absently. The moon shone in his eyes, which were glowing blank as snow. As the tractor chugged on he began to pray. He stammered out one Lord's Prayer after another, until the first of the village houses came into sight. To this day the people in the village are convinced that that burial was his undoing. The dandified Communist wasn't the only one that night to feel the full measure of the fear that lies inside us all. Once the devil had them bagged up, his two hired thugs also heard the bell toll. The driver started going to church and would talk about what happened the night of the burial to anybody who'd listen. The Perfumed Commissar was transferred out of the district. The rumor that the driver not only buried the horse but had poisoned it as well never died down. The man disappeared for a while, and people in the village thought he had been arrested, as he deserved to be. But he showed up later on, and a few days after that he was missing his right hand. Since everyone in that village knew him he wanted to disappear, so he applied for the job of sexton in another village, and was taken on. There he told people he had lost his hand during the war. The hand itself turned up in the flour bin in his kitchen after he had moved away. For some years after the war, only cripples were taken on as sextons, so he had hacked off his own hand.

Paul was making coffee, water was hissing on the stove, and a blackbird flew up to the kitchen window, settled on the metal ledge, and pecked at its own shadow.

There used to be two of them, said Paul, but then one day ⊓ saw one lying near the front door covered with ants.

Paul stirred the coffee, the spoon clinked, I put my forefinger to my lips.

Shhh.

No, we can go on talking, it'll fly away in a minute anyway.

But he laid down the spoon without a sound. On the table in front of my hands: the red coffee tin, the jam the color of egg yolk, and the white slices of bread. Outside the sheer wall of sky, the pale yellow beak and the feathers made of pitch. Everything was looking at everything else. Paul poured the coffee into the cups, the steam drifted up to his neck. I tapped the cup and pointed a hot finger to the window—the blackbird flew away, the coffee was still too hot.

The Perfumed Commissar, I said, was transferred to the nursery gardens, where he remained. But the effect of the white horse has not worn off, to this day he's above being a foot soldier and hasn't had to do a stroke of work. They couldn't use him in a top managerial position or as a worker, so they made him a supervisor, and that's what he's remained. He learned the Latin plant names by heart till he could rattle them off fluently as prayers. On Sundays he would go for walks with his wife, daughter, and son, and later with me too. He'd break off a small stick—it had to be a straight one—strip the leaves, point it at some periwinkle growing by the path and say *Vinca minor,* and reel off everything he knew about the plant. Next to a bench he'd say *Aruncus dioicus,* and tell us everything he knew about goatsbeard. And on the next path *Epimedium rubrum* and *plumbagum.* His *Hosta fortunei* grew beside a hollow. You were expected to stop and listen. My husband told me he used to be even stricter. If he or his sister laughed, he wouldn't speak to them for days. During my last summer with them, I was going to fetch some daisies from the back garden to put in a vase. I saw my father-in-law talking out loud to himself by the walnut tree, not only saying the words but using his hands and even stamping his feet. He was completely absorbed and didn't notice me till I was right beside him. He realized I must have been watching him, gave an unembarrassed smile, and asked me what I should have asked him:

Has the sun given you a headache.

No, I was going to pick some daisies.

Are you really all right.

Yes, how about you.

How about me, my nose is still in the middle of my face, isn't it.

So is mine, but you ask me all the same.

I can't complain, he said.

I wondered whether there were two versions of him—one close up and peaceful, the other far off and full of dead people murmuring. To chase them away he had to shake off his burden. In secret, if he could. Or if that wasn't possible, then openly, but in terms designed to make people admire rather than pity him. And the best way to manage that was dancing. There were only the two of us at home, he and I. My husband and mother-in-law had gone into town on some errand that afternoon. I never did pick any more daisies, not for fear of him, but because I was afraid of the white daisies.

He worked in the garden but all the Latin names in the world couldn't give him a green thumb; apart from grafting roses, he hadn't learned a thing from working in the nursery. Two years ago they received an important order, a factory director had died and there was a big state funeral, the nursery was to furnish twenty wreaths as big as cartwheels. My father-in-law wanted to make an impression and use something special. So he prescribed tiger lilies and ferns instead of the traditional carnation and ivy wreaths. But what they unloaded from the car at the Heroes' Cemetery was nothing but a lot of wilted brown stalks. Thirty years in the business and he didn't even know that tiger lilies wilt within half an hour. He should have been sacked, but he had the chief engineer on his side. Twenty-eight years younger than he, she was well-built, fresh out of school, full of energy, and could run around nonstop and give orders better than he could. The working days were long, the sky warm, the summer green. As June turned to July and the foliage grew thick on the shrubs, my father-in-law started fondling the new chief engineer. She didn't protest, either. There weren't very many aphids or mites that year, so they had time for each other. Comrade Louse Inspector convinced the director of the funeral service that tiger lilies generally have a long life. She said that all the talk in specialist circles that summer was of a form of mildew from the south of France that attacked cemeteries, since graves aren't sprayed out of respect for the dead. When freshly cut flowers come into contact with this mildew, they wither in no time at all, every last one of them. Exactly the same thing would have happened with carnations, she told the director. And he put his faith in her expertise, for his own, although he was about to retire, also barely extended beyond the difference between chamomiles and carnations.

I'd really like to know how many people from our apartment block, from the shops down below, from the factory, or from the whole city have ever been summoned. Albu's office building must have something going on every day of the week, behind every door in the corridor. I can't see the man with the briefcase who ran off to find his aspirin. Maybe the tram left without him, or maybe it was too full for him to get back on. He'll just have to wait for the next one—if he has the time. A woman has sat down beside me, her behind is broader than the seat, what's more she's sitting with her legs astride a bag. Her thigh is rubbing against me, she rummages in her bag and pulls out a little cone made of newspaper. It's soggy and full of blood-red bumps—cherries, of all things, cherries. She reaches in with one hand and spits the stones into the other. She doesn't linger over each individual cherry, she doesn't suck them clean, she leaves a little meat on every stone. What's her rush, nobody's going to swipe her cherries and gobble them up. I wonder if she's ever been summoned for questioning, or whether she might be sometime in the future. Her hand is soon so full of cherry stones she can't close her fingers. She can drop them inconspicuously on the floor, even spit them out for all I care. There are people standing in the aisle all the way up to the driver, it probably wouldn't bother them, either. The driver won't discover the stones until this evening, he'll be annoyed because he has to sweep out the car, but there'll be plenty of other things left over from the day's run, too. What on earth was the old officer thinking of with Lilli. Cherry season comes every year and lasts from May through September, and it'll be that way as long as the world exists, no matter what. How does that help him, there aren't any cherries in prison. It's good the car's so crowded, I'll have more than enough space when I get to Albu's. And on the way back, if I do come home today. The trams don't run so often in the evening. I'll wait, climb on board along with a few others, and sit down in that awful yellow light. Maybe some of them will have a few cherries later on, a few after dessert, for instance. As far as I'm concerned, they can go right ahead.

It wasn't until two days later that I went to my landlord. I paid him what I owed, two thousand lei. The skin on his hands was as thin as the skin on his face. I counted the notes right into the palm of his hand, and he pretended he was counting them in his head but in fact you could hear him whispering. One crumpled note fell on the floor, I picked it up but didn't smooth it out. I put it back in his hand, upside down, and noticed that the landlord had a weak grip. The old man was even worse at taking than I had been at the flea market. What was he thinking about when he said:

Oh Lord, my hands are dirty from peeling potatoes, I'm making mashed potatoes today. Do you like mashed potatoes.

I've already eaten.

With schnitzel and salad.

At that moment I saw he had a wooden handle sticking out of his jacket pocket, it belonged to a knife. When I'd rung the bell, he'd slipped the potato knife in his pocket instead of leaving it in the kitchen. Either because he was expecting somebody and wanted to keep the knife handy or because he forgot he was holding it and only when he was about to open the door did he realize that a knife could alarm a visitor. I quickly handed him the money so I could be on my way. But then we struck a deal. He smiled and chirped and bought the refrigerator and carpets off me for a hundred more than I had paid him. He went back to the kitchen for the extra money. And when he returned with the additional hundred lei, the knife was still in his jacket, either because he'd forgotten it or wanted to keep it handy.

I'm moving in with a man and a motorcycle, I said.

The one from the flea market, he said.

You know him, I asked.

If it's the same one.

Were you at the flea market too.

And at the game preserve, he said. I won't look for a new tenant until winter, the room will be more expensive then. Not for you, if it doesn't work out, you can come back.

Is that why you bought the carpets and the refrigerator.

I bought them because I needed to.

For a moment I thought he said: Because I needed you. I said:

I'll be living in the leaning tower.

He knew where that was.

My first morning in the leaning tower, Paul and I talked and talked till the sun was at high noon. I was amazed at all the mothers and fathers we had to bring in just to explain where we were each coming from on our way to meeting the other. Handkerchiefs, strollers, baby carriages, peach trees, cuff links, ants—even dust and wind carried weight. It's easy to talk about bad years if they are past. But when you have to say who you are right at this very moment, it's hard to get more out than an uneasy silence.

That afternoon Paul went to the shop and bought himself a bottle of yellow-green buffalo-grass vodka. The sun was going west, the vodka was going straight to Paul's head. An ant scurried across the kitchen table, Paul waved a match over it.

Where do the ants go, to the forest.
Where has the forest gone, into wood.
Where has the wood gone, into fire.
Where has the fire gone, into my heart.

Suddenly the match flared alight. It was black magic, because Paul was holding the box in his other hand under the table. The match curled up, the flame licked at his thumb. Paul blew, looked into the thread of smoke.

My heart has stopped,
and the ants keep going.

Paul wasn't drunk, only tipsy. He was high, but it was more an external thing. Having ants go marching through your heart is no laughing matter as far as I'm concerned, but Paul laughed out loud so that even my tongue started to tickle. Paul's light-headedness was contagious, back then there wasn't any trace of darkness in the vodka, and I wasn't afraid of his drinking. Paul didn't drink that much during the first six months—by the end of the evening half the blade of grass would still be wet. And during the first few weeks, when he came home from work he went straight out onto the balcony and his aerials: the sparks that fly when you're welding and how quickly they fade.

Where has the fire gone, I always saw the match and the ants in our hearts. Now and then Paul would whistle to himself, a song so out of tune it sounded more like grinding metal than music. Each week he'd finish a whole antler of an aerial—and then there were nearly enough for a Sunday at the flea market and a heap of money. But Paul never got the chance to sell them. Two young men came knocking at the door.

Black-marketeering, they said. And infiltration of the state through foreign TV channels.

Without asking, they packed all the tools and iron tubing into some sacks they'd brought along and carried them down on the elevator to a small truck that we could see from the kitchen window. They left the finished aerials out in the stairwell. Paul said:

Once you've got everything, close the door behind you.

He took the brandy into the kitchen and locked himself in. I sat leaning against the wall in the stairwell so as not to be in the way and watched the two men at work. They carried the aerials down the stairs, without taking the elevator, two at a time, one in each hand. A quick clatter of steps and then the echo, wary poachers with stolen antlers. They never left each other's side, together they came and went three times. On their last trip one of them snorted with exertion, I saw his shirt was sticking to his back, and he said:

We have to.

Do your job, I said, just don't tell me any stories.

I let them take away all the antlers, then they were gone and I had to pound on the kitchen door before Paul opened it. The brandy was gone and Paul was pacing back and forth between the main room and the balcony with more feet than he had, and shouted:

That spy is sitting over there and watching.

In the apartment tower opposite, two stories down, a woman was sitting on the balcony and sewing.

Let her sew, she can't see up to here.

She can sew wherever she likes, but not on the balcony.

That's her balcony, she's not interested in you.

We'll see about that, said Paul.

He staggered back into the room and fetched a chair. He stood on it like an ungainly child. While I was wondering what he was doing and holding on to him so he wouldn't fall, he dropped his trousers and began pissing off the balcony down into the street. The woman gathered up her sewing and went inside.

At the motor factory there was a meeting because of Paul's stolen iron tubing, he got the sack. His fellow workers from the assembly division sat silently in the back—like piles of shit in the bushes, as Paul put it. They've all stolen things and they still do. At home they make watering cans, coffee grinders, immersion coils, irons, crimping irons, curling tongs, and sell them for good money. Every other one of them is a Nelu, you don't have to write notes, they have other ways.

Paul wasn't summoned, but neither was he spared. When I moved in with him it was like breaking and entering into his daily rhythm. They would have tracked down anything carrying my scent, and nobody who was connected with me would be overlooked. Paul was being punished together with me. Even on the days when I wasn't summoned, they trampled on my heart, because they were after Paul. It was he who had the accident and not me. The outcome might be the same regardless of whether they were threatening his life because of me or because they felt he deserved it. But it isn't the same. Before the accident, Paul found it harder to take the waiting than I did. I used to wait for him to come home from his drinking. He, on the other hand, would wait for me to return from being summoned. Since the accident, however, the waiting is the same for us both.

If I search my brain for all the people I know with combs, there are just two I could really trust. In Lilli's case it no longer matters. Only Paul is left. I can see what you're thinking, the Major says. In that case I ought to be able to tell by looking whether somebody's been summoned, at least whether my neighbors have. Maybe they know all about my connection with Albu and just don't want to reveal what they know.

Old Micu who lives downstairs by the entrance told me last September that he'd been summoned in April.

Because of you, he said.

As if it was my fault. When I moved into the leaning tower with Paul, he was very formal with me, calling me Miss and by my last name. Ever since he was summoned, and because it was my fault, he just calls me You. He used to work as a chauffeur for the director of the shoe factory. Because he's so muscular Paul thinks he was some sort of bodyguard as well. Frau Micu was a secretary at the music school. They have two sons who rarely write and never visit. Paul frequently talks to Herr Micu, more about Frau Micu than about himself or Herr Micu. She's the same age as her husband and since they retired is always at home. Herr Micu spends all day hanging around the entrance or walking up and down the row of shops looking for people to talk to.

That time he was sitting by the entrance on the steps, eating freshly washed blue grapes when I came home. He stood up and accompanied me inside, his grapes dripping all the way to the elevator. Not until I had pressed the button and the cables had begun to rumble somewhere upstairs did he tell me that he had been summoned because of me.

Why did you go, I asked. I have to go because I got summoned on my own account. I wouldn't go because of others.

You expect me to believe that, he said.

With his thumb and middle finger he pulled the grapes off faster than I could count. His mouth was up against my ear, and every grape squirted juice when he bit it. He kept his little finger sticking out, an affectation that makes a man like him, whose false teeth squeak as he eats, even more unattractive. Did I want a few grapes, he asked, since I couldn't take my eyes off his hand.

I'm not reproaching you for anything, he said.

What do you want, then.

I also have children.

Never take children into your confidence, I said.

The elevator came and the door opened. It was empty, but Herr Micu stuck his head inside as if to double-check whether someone wasn't standing on the ceiling. He wedged his foot against the door.

I waited to catch you because I had no idea when you come and when you go. I have to write it down.

I could see the last mailbox on the wall reflected in one of his eyes, or was that just his pupil turning white and square. I didn't compare it with his other eye, because he whispered:

I've already filled two school notebooks, I have to buy them myself.

He'd torn off all the grapes, scraps of blue peel were still stuck to each thin stalk on the cluster. Then he looked along the mailboxes toward the entrance.

I haven't said anything to you, I swore I wouldn't, what do I mean swore, it's all written down in black and white.

Frau Micu's been playing the lottery for half her life. After she retired, she started gambling more and more. She's always known that one day she'd win a huge fortune. And the further off that day gets, the more fervent her belief. Every Wednesday when the numbers are drawn she waits in her red flowery Sunday dress. Her brown patent-leather shoes are standing by in the hall so she can slip them on when the lottery man rings the bell. Usually no one rings at all on Wednesdays, because by now everyone in the block is well aware what a significant day it is. And if the bell does ring, then it's only the postman or a forgetful neighbor. Then Frau Micu, dressed in her Sunday best, slowly closes the door and feels that, once again, she has been betrayed. Her world collapses, she buries her face in the armchair and sobs. Herr Micu smashes a couple of plates against the wall and sweeps up the pieces. Then he gets a grip on himself and comforts her. Soon the local radio station starts its pop music hit parade. The week goes by and it all blows over, until the following Wednesday, when the whole cycle begins once again. Paul's often heard her crying inside the apartment and has asked Herr Micu how he stands it. Herr Micu talked about another cross he has to bear. Just like earlier, when he was still a chauffeur and she was a secretary, he got used to her poking around the school and searching all over town for what she called rubies but were really just broken pieces of red glass. She's always had an artistic streak, he said. Once she'd filled her first box of rubies, she took it to the city museum and then to a goldsmith. Ultimately she threatened to commit suicide, so Herr Micu sent her to a watchmaker, after having first bought the man a few drinks at the tavern, so that someone would finally confirm to his wife that it really was rubies in her box. The business with the Sunday dress will never change, Wednesday evening it will be hung back up in silence and now and then tears will be shed. But there's no more talk of suicide. The watchmaker was worth it, Herr Micu says, I'd have spared myself a good deal of trouble if I'd thought of that earlier.

Shortly after I moved to the tower block, I saw Frau Micu leaning against the wall behind the entrance. She was in her stocking feet, wearing a housecoat. Her cheeks were shining with a fuzzy down that thickened into a belt of tattered fur around her chin: a thin mustache ran above her lips and curled upward under each nostril. Frau Micu was sucking on her index finger and wiping spittle around her eyes, the way cats wash themselves. I walked to the elevator. Without moving from the spot she called out:

Miss.

She showed me a piece of red glass.

Have you ever seen such a big ruby.

Never, I said.

That would be something for the Queen of England, I think I'll send it to her, what do you think.

What if it gets stolen in the mail.

You're right, she said, and put it away in the pocket of her dress.

She must have known something about Herr Micu's written observations. Long before her husband took me into his confidence, I came home from town one afternoon and found her standing right in the entrance hall. She was wearing a dishcloth as a shawl. She held out an arm to block my way and said:

First you went out and then Paul. But then only Paul showed up.

And now I'm back too, I said.

After Paul showed up, she said, and when Radu showed up he weighed four kilos, and then Emil weighed four and a quarter.

I'm not counting Mara, my husband didn't want her. And then I had Emil again, twice, that's not possible, but back then you were allowed to have twins separately.

She no longer knew the difference between a dishcloth and a shawl. But she knew what her children had weighed at birth, just as my grandfather knew the measurements of the bricks in the camp.

Partly out of spite because he was writing down my comings and goings and heaven knows what else, and partly out of gratitude that he had confided in me, I bought a school notebook for Herr Micu. I wanted him to feel jittery by making him write down his observations in something I had given him. I wanted to throw a monkey wrench in the works, politely, because quarreling got you nowhere. It wasn't Wednesday, so I rang the bell and Herr Micu opened the door, holding a slice of bread and drippings, sprinkled with gleaming grains of salt. He shook his head.

Much too big.

I didn't know.

Mine are smaller and thicker.

Why can't you write in a bigger one, I said.

It has to fit into my jacket pocket, he said, no, no.

Since then I've used the notebook to record whatever Albu says to me while kissing my hand, or how many paving stones, fence slats, telegraph poles, or windows there are between one spot and another. I don't like writing, because something that's written down can be discovered, but I have to do it. Often the same things, in the same place, change their number from one day to the next. At first glance everything looks exactly the same, but not when you count it. Or when you play the sketching game, closing your eyes and using your finger to outline clouds, roofs, the leaves trembling on trees, or the forks in branches if the trees are bare. The higher the object, the easier it is to trace. I've often drawn the church steeple this way, all the way to the very tip, and the tall tenements right up to the weather vanes. I sketch Paul's aerials, which look like antlers even when they're on the roofs, without leaving out a single branch. But I only focus on his and no others. I used to pick up little stones from the edge of the path to help me practice sketching. Ever since I found the parcel wrapped like candy in my bag, I use my fore-finger, crooking and twisting it to follow the contours. I didn't check whether the severed finger could be bent.

I once sketched Lilli this way. She was standing in the entrance stairwell at the factory, a whole flight of stairs above me, and turned so I could see her profile. I showed her how straight her forehead was, the way her nose stood above the world, the milky white color of her chin and throat—like frosted glass. Even at that distance my finger could feel the dif-ference between Lilli's skin and other objects. When I reached the angle of her shoulder, Lilli placed her hands on her breasts:

Make me transparent, she said, I'm sure you can do that.

I couldn't, I only sketched the side closest to me, her rear arm was hidden when Lilli said:

Now it's your turn.

We never got around to it, we heard steps in the corridor, Lilli ran down the stairs. Her sandals had only two slender straps, her ankles were nimble, her dress fluttered. From below, Lilli's thighs went all the way up to her throat. In the yard we giggled, she louder than me, but then she was crying, in fact she might have been crying from the moment she started gig-gling. I took a gulp of air and she laughed for real, dried her eyes, and said:

It's only water. Do you remember Anton, who sold leather goods.

The one with the wart on the side of his nose.

No, that was the photographer.

The one who moved to the country.

Yes. He had water in his lungs, and it didn't clear up. He died here in the hospital, the day before yesterday, I didn't know a thing about it. Do you remember how we were caught.

No, I'd even forgotten his name was Anton.

There was a knock at the door, it was two inspectors, I was in my underwear. They gulped just like you did right now. They sat down on a pile of leather jackets, rested their chins on their hands, and whispered to each other. And Anton started holding leather skirts up to me as if I was a customer. He kept trying bigger and bigger skirts, making sure none of them actually fit me. Then he measured my hip size in hand spans, my backside, and the length halfway down to my knee. If you're as slim as this one, you only need one calfskin to make a skirt, he said, winking at the inspectors. He wrote down the measurements in centimeters on a chocolate box that had been lying there ever since I knew him, and he shoved the pencil behind his ear. You don't have any stomach to speak of, two darts in back will do it, that's it, no other seam. Then he passed around the chocolates. One of the inspectors took a handful, and his companion told Anton to take a walk for an hour. As for me, they wanted me to stay. Anton closed the chocolate box and threw the two of them out, saying:

I'd sooner kill the pair of you.

That's why he had to move out to the country.

Would you have liked to keep on going.

Yes.

But at the time you said, Now I've got him off my back.

And that was true.

But then you missed him after all.

Not in the slightest, Lilli said.

The cherry eater sitting next to me found a space in her crowded bag where she could drop all the stones, she crumpled up the newspaper cone and crammed it inside. She wiped her hands against each other and then on her dress. The stains don't show against the red flower pattern. I see an arm reaching up toward the handrail, holding the briefcase, now I see a head as well. Where has he been hiding all this time—he obviously managed to make it back onto the tram after all. So he doesn't have as much free time as I thought. Or maybe the pushing and shoving doesn't bother him. Some people get pushy in the hope of starting a fight. And there are plenty of dodderers who just let people walk right over them without saying a word. The cherry eater has stood up and squeezed herself into the aisle. I have to get off at the next stop too, a lot of people are getting off there. The long-distance buses are waiting around the corner. All the people with baskets, cans, and bags are getting out at the Central Bus Station to travel on to their villages. The man with the briefcase is getting out there as well, either to continue on to the country or else because he lives in the neighborhood. It's possible we're headed in the same direction, he may even work at the place where I've been summoned. Or maybe he's just moving to the door now in order to get out several stops later—a lot of people do that. The cherry eater smiles at me with dark blue gums. She pushes through to the door at the back. If I have to I'll push my way to the front door, it's a little closer. Is the woman planning to plant her cherry stones. My grandfather said there are wild seeds in the Baragan Steppe that won't germinate unless a bird eats them and shits them out. But cherry stones have to dry in the sun before they're planted, otherwise they won't grow into trees. If all her stones were to grow, she'd be carrying a cherry orchard home in her bag. The passengers are leaning forward, backward, all together, the bag with the stones right in their middle. The driver rings the bell and shouts out the window: You want to die, why don't you go to your bedroom instead of loafing around here on the tracks. Then he shouts into the car: Does every idiot have to get up in the morning. Is the driver talking to himself or to all of us. Besides, what does he know: I for one would be happy to stay in bed, although there's no question that Albu gets up in the morning.

In the evenings when I'd walk home from the bus depot it would be so dark I couldn't make out anything beyond the avenue at first, then my eyes would grow used to the night and I would see more and more. I would count the entryways to the apartment buildings, blended together and then separated as the same long building went on and on and the numbers above the entrances grew and grew. When I turned onto our street, I would outline the roof of the bread factory, holding a little stone in my hand, recovering every weather vane and chimney from the falling night, in order to counter the deceit of the entryways. I had tried counting to distract myself from the dark, out of boredom. But the numbers preferred my being confused to my being secure. So before they could turn the entire street against me I played at tracing things. After I saw the woman with the braid on the bus, I stopped distracting myself by counting entryways, and the time passed anyway. Except that one day, after I'd already been away from the small town so long that I no longer recognized the weather vanes on the bread factory, I turned onto a side street behind the post office and said to myself:

Keep those stubs on the table.

It started to rain. A man walking in front of me opened his umbrella, and I stopped where I was. When the umbrella reached the other end of the street and dwindled to the size of a hat, I traced it with my finger and the sketching started all over again. Keep those stubs on the table, Albu had said, because I'd been twisting the large button on my blouse. I placed my hands on the table but forgot to keep them there and he said it again. That was the day Albu found a hair on my shoulder. He grazed his fingers across my cheek as he took it. His cologne smelled very close, the smoothly shaven pores under his chin, with smaller and smaller specks running up his cheeks like polished wood. He held the hair in two fingers and stretched out his three others and was about to let it fall to the floor. He can do what he wants to any hair on my head, wrap them around his index finger and pull me wherever he wants. But if a hair has fallen out it should stay where it is. Albu was almost certainly after something else when he stood up and pulled his shirt cuff over his watch. He would never have even seen a hair on Lilli's shoulder. Has he finally forgotten what he's after, as I have the name of his bitter perfume, or has he decided on a different tactic. But I could never mistake the smell of his cologne, whether it's called Avril or Septembre, I twisted my large button again and said:

Put the hair back, it belongs to me.

I was startled at the nerve in my own voice, after I spoke I figured I'd be punished. He curled his fingers back in and stared at the pattern of holes stenciled in the tips of his shoes— probably to decide what to do next. And I stared at the light coming through the window. Over there lay the nibbled pencil, and Albu's fingers were on my shoulder. He actually did put the hair back. Then he yelled:

Keep those stubs on the table.

He stood at the window with his back to me, shaking his head, in the glare his hair looked like a fine big mane that covered his neck. He laughed out loud in the direction of the tree, turned to face me, and sat down on the windowsill. He rested one shoe on its heel so the tip was pointing straight up, revealing the clean sole, and couldn't stop laughing. A laughing fit just like the ones I had. His ear looked green, taken into possession by the foliage. What was he laughing about, the greenish tinge prefigured his passing from the world, not mine. A little wind, and the tree would have drowned out that fit of laughter. In his place I wouldn't have laughed just then.

Now the tram is at the bus station, everyone is shoving and I'm standing in the middle of the car. The man with the briefcase shouts over the passengers to the driver: Jesus Christ, take a look at all these stupid people. And the man behind him scratches his chin and says: Watch it, silkworm, or I'll curl your mustache with my heel and you'll be taking your teeth home in your handkerchief. The man with the briefcase doesn't have a mustache but the man who just spoke does. Now both of them are outside. The man with the briefcase is facing the roughneck, who wags his forefinger as if threatening a child and gives a coarse laugh. His arms are long and muscular, his teeth white, he means business. Before the day's over he'll have found someone he can beat senseless. The man with the briefcase thinks he's above getting into a fight like that, better to get away in one piece than risk bloodying your clothes—even if the price is a bit of humiliation. And the blood would be his, since in the heat of his rage he was bound to be defeated. So he shrugs his shoulders and saunters off in the opposite direction from me. It turns out he doesn't work where I've been summoned. A pity, if he did at least I'd know someone there, maybe not very well, but at least differently than the way I know Albu. Someone who'd let himself be humiliated, who'd been trodden into the dust and didn't do a thing about it. The driver yells: Let's go or it'll be Christmas before I get out of here. The cherry eater's already outside, she walks to a bin and tosses the crumpled paper bag inside. Some man throws a cap in through the window, right in the driver's face. The man's hair is tangled, his trousers are wet with piss, his shirt is bloody. He has a fresh gash on his forehead. He has a large sack next to him that's tied tight but is squirming around. The driver tosses the cap back out the window: Keep your lice. Hold on to it for me, would you, the man laughs, I'm getting in. Not in here you're not, the conductor says, I'm not a toilet cleaner, this is a streetcar. I'm a father, the man says, reeling, since seven minutes past two last night, I have a son, my wife's at the maternity hospital. And what's in the sack, the driver asks. A lamb, the man says, I'm going to give it to the doctor and kiss his golden hands. The man fumbles with his cap but can't find his head, so he stuffs the cap into his pants pocket. Out of the question, the driver says, if your son pissed in my car I wouldn't kick him out since he can't even walk yet. But that doesn't go for you. The man drags his sack across the rails and pushes against the door. The passengers getting out push him away with their elbows. The man plants one foot squarely on the step. The driver gets up and pushes him down. He falls. Hey, boss, better not leave me here, you better take me with you, may your son go blind . . . The driver spits on the step, shuts the door, and drives off. The lamb in the sack cries out briefly, perhaps the wheels passed over it. On either side of me are people who wanted to get off, but no one says a word. The driver says: I'll let you all off at the next stop—it's not far. That's easy for him to say, but now I'll have to hurry. At the next stop it's already a quarter to ten.

It's possible to take long strides, to walk and breathe at the same time. You can't look down at your shoes or up in the air—otherwise things might start to blur. You have to keep looking all around just as if you were moving slowly, you can make almost as much progress that way as running, yet you don't exhaust yourself. But for me to walk like that I'd have to have a clear path ahead, the two people in front of me would have to let me pass. They're carrying watermelons in a mesh bag that's swinging back and forth between them, blocking the way. Each melon has been notched open. Probably whoever sold them cut a wedge, which he then raised to his lips using the tip of his knife. After tasting each one he plugged it back inside the melon. All these melons must be ripe. Notched melons are quick to ferment, you have to eat them the same day. Do these two have such a big family. Or do they propose to eat nothing but melons morning, noon, and night, five cold melons, with bread so as to avoid diarrhea or a fit of the shivers. Warm melons taste of mud, they have to be chilled. No refrigerator will hold five melons, the best they can do is a bathtub. My grandfather said:

People used to leave melons in their wells. The water bears them up easily, they float. After an hour you can fish them out with a bucket and eat them. At the first bite your mouth hurts as if you were eating snow, but then your tongue gets used to it. Overchilled melons are a trap, they're mealy sweet, you eat too much, your stomach freezes. Every summer people died from eating those melons out of their wells, even in town.

Nobody dies from eating melons out of the tub, although many people die in the bath. Yes, you can have a warm soak in the mornings, chill melons at noon, and slaughter lambs and geese in the afternoon, rinse away the blood, and then take another warm wash in the evenings. All in the same tub. And when you've had your fill of melon, lamb, goose, and yourself, then you can fill up the tub one last time and drown yourself in it, my grandfather said, Oh yes, you can do all that.

I'd rather do it in the river, I said.

But right here there isn't any river. You'd have to drive off looking for one, and by the time they pull you out they probably won't know who you were. Corpses fished out of rivers are gruesome. Anyone that fed up with life is better off laying out one last set of clean clothes and dying a pleasant death at home, in the bath.

If you count their shadows, there are four of them doing the carrying. Sometimes people need only one melon but they take more because they're so cheap. They think they're saving money, and then they let the melons spoil. I walk close behind the mesh bag, making noise to announce my presence, but the cars are louder. Why are they pulling the bag so far apart, it doesn't make it any lighter.

Excuse me.

No, they can't hear me, I need to say more than that.

Climbing roses are planted between the houses, the tall dill in the vegetable beds is flowering in the wind, while the fritillarias are sluggish, girding themselves for the heat of the day, the dust makes them drowsy. Clotheslines are stretched between the fruit trees, lots of peach and quince. Housecoats and aprons, still wet in dark patches, catch the dust before they're dry. I've never been here before, not even aimlessly. Lilli's blue skirt with the accordion pleats belongs here, where the gardens are too small for large trees. If he wants to get annoyed, that's his business, I tug at the melon man's sleeve.

Excuse me, I have to get past.

He turns his head and trots on another couple paces and then turns around again. Then he lets go of the bag.

What are you doing, she yells, can't you say something if you're going to let go.

She pulls her shoe out from under the melons, takes her foot out of her shoe, then strips off a bandage that's slipped off her little toe:

Well, isn't that great, now the blister has burst.

Hey, the man says, look at this, we know her.

His brown dyed hair has a silvery sheen close to the scalp, the way it did after the night had been danced away and the light was glaring and Martin no longer counted as part of the paraputch. And her face is lopsided, the way it was after Martin had treated her so horribly in the bathroom.

Oh, Anastasia says, your hair is short.

What are you doing with five melons.

You've counted them, he laughs, we're celebrating, you can imagine where.

I imagined the paraputch.

And how are you, she asks.

Fine, I say.

So are we, he says, maybe we'll get together sometime.

Maybe, I say.

A truck roars by, Anastasia says:

We better get going.

Then Martin kisses my hand in farewell, and I turn toward the street, where two baby shoes are dangling by their laces right in front of a driver's forehead. And when the car moves past I see an open garage across the street, an old man wearing shorts, and a red Java. And who should be coming out of the back garden, ducking under the clothesline and heading into the garage but Paul. By Anastasia's watch it is five past ten.

Paul and the old man are laughing, I look to see if his thin legs have marble veins and check the aerial on the roof. It's one of Paul's. Paul picks up a wrench without even having to look for it, he just reaches over to the shelf. In the evening, when he claimed to be out drinking, I believed him. Why not, his being drunk was real enough, no deceit there. I never asked who he was drinking with or who was paying. Why would I. At home Paul drinks by himself. After the accident he said:

Drinkers recognize each other right away, from one table to the next, by their looks, the way the glasses speak to each other. I don't want anything to do with drinking buddies. I'll drink with others, but I prefer to sit by myself.

But then Paul threw our bedding out the window into the night, beginning with our pillows. I saw them lying down below, white and small like two handkerchiefs. I laughed as I took the elevator down, barefoot, and brought them back up. By the time I was back with the pillows, the quilts were down on the ground. And when I brought those back up, I was crying because they were so big, and because I had given in to some fool's nighttime whim. Herr Micu's bedroom window was dimly lit by a bedside lamp. It was late but still Wednesday, the day of the weekly lottery disaster. Who knows what kind of consolation Herr Micu was doling out to get his wife to accept the next day, maybe sex, a bit of physical love.

Young men tire you out, Lilli said, but older men can make women's flesh light and smooth during sex.

Throwing bedding out the window was physical too. It wasn't love, but it was more physical than throwing out dresses. The Sunday dress that Frau Micu had worn on Wednesday as she waited to become rich was now back in the closet. But she was still wearing her body. When Frau Micu leans on the wall inside the entryway, not knowing herself as she is now but convinced she knows who she was twenty years ago, I want to run away. Her sad flesh doesn't face the sun oblivious to the world, the way my Mama's did, it looks ready to be touched. Herr Micu once said to Paul:

Every time we have sex it's a spoonful of sugar for her shattered nerves, the only thing I can use to keep my wife from taking leave of her senses.

Her senses, Paul asked.

Her senses, I said taking leave of her senses, I'm not saying I can restore her mind.

If the bedside lamp was lit not for sex but to light the day's final entry in the notebook, I didn't want his pen to witness the quilts and pillows. I didn't turn on the light in the entrance hall but carried the things to the elevator like a thief. When I got upstairs with the quilts, Paul was lying on the white pillow in his pajamas like a striped piece of paper. He pulled his knees up to his stomach and asked:

Did anyone see you.

I covered him up, then laid the second quilt on my part of the bed and smoothed the creases, as if on the cloth lay the woman I wanted to be from tomorrow on—one who would no longer put up with any mad drunkenness. Paul looked up at the bedroom ceiling and said:

I'm sorry.

I'd never heard anything like that before. Not even when an apology was grinding his teeth or twisting his mouth—he always kept them bottled up inside his face, he never let them out. What earthly connection could there have been between that and the next day, when I thought up a lie and stepped out of the noisy row of shops into the stillness of the pharmacy carrying a mesh bag full of potatoes and said:

My grandfather caught a splinter in the eye when he was chopping wood and he's lost it, the right eye. He lives a long way away and can't come to town. He hasn't been out of the house since, not even to church or the hairdresser's. He's ashamed to be seen, I'd like to buy him a glass eye.

There's nothing to worry about if you're lying about the dead—none of it can come true. With good lies, with Albu, I know when it's working because from one word to the next I believe it myself. Chopping wood was pretty lame, I've told so many lies out of fear and for others that if there's no fear, or when it's just for myself, I can't do it. The pharmacist stood there wearing her own dress under her white coat, like two women, one inside the other, an older and a younger version. The woman in the dress knew pain, the woman in the coat knew how to treat it. But neither one knew how to gauge a good lie. Nevertheless, the pharmacist lowered her eyes and said:

You can buy one even without a prescription. Don't worry, it'll fit. You can't exchange it, though. Pick one out of the window. You can have two if you want.

She laughed.

Even three, God knows there are enough of them there collecting dust.

I took a dark blue glass eye, now there was a gap in the display. My grandfather had brown eyes with that subdued gleam you can't get with glass because it hasn't suffered. The eye I bought was a plum in water, but the water was ice. An eye that wanted to match Lilli's but fell short of being amazing. Of course no hand or machine could have even come close to capturing her tobacco flower nose.

Before I bought the potatoes I had been to the candy section in the grocery store. In glass jars stacked on top of each other I saw dead wasps clinging to red candies, then rusty razor blades, then broken cookies, then boxes of matches, then green candies stuck together, also with wasps. And the bottles along the shelf against the wall alternated in color, milky-yellow egg liqueur, pink raspberry juice, greenish rubbing alcohol, nail polish remover as clear as water. Each item seemed to think it was really something else. The shop assistant gave the impression of a person put together with matches, razor blades, candy stuck together with wasps, and cookies, all on the verge of falling apart.

A hundred grams of the sweet razor blades, I said.

You better get out of here, he yelled. Go buy something at the pharmacy that'll get you your wits back.

It was true, all the goods were addling my brain. I went to the greengrocer's and was glad that the potatoes, as they went from the crate onto the scales, didn't turn into shoes or stones. I was holding three kilos of potatoes and my head was full of the irreversibility of things. Then I went into the pharmacy and bought the glass eye. Once they stop summoning me, Paul can attach a little ring to it and I'll wear it as a necklace. So I thought at the time.

Whenever I hear the elevator descending to fetch Albu's henchmen, I can hear his voice quietly in my head: Tuesday at ten sharp, Saturday at ten sharp, Thursday at ten sharp. How often, after closing the door, have I said to Paul:

I'm not going there anymore.

Paul would hold me in his arms and say:

If you don't go, they'll come and fetch you, and then they'll have you for good.

And I would nod.

Now Paul is setting his handkerchief on the ground next to the motorbike. He sits down on it and tightens screws. And I'm standing behind a bush and don't want to budge, don't want to go click-click across the asphalt all the way back to the leaning tower that everyone knows. Except Frau Micu, who never walks more than the ten paces from her apartment to the elevator and the ten to the entrance and not a step further because she forgets the way. She once said:

The world's a big place, how can I smell where our apartment is from outside.

About the elevator she said:

You step into the car, it's powered by this cable, not gasoline. You better have a ticket since it's the first day of the month and the checkers are bound to stop by today. You'll starve up there on the roof.

She handed me an apricot, I went into the elevator. The stone was pulsing through the flesh of the fruit warmed by her hand. Upstairs I threw the apricot out the window as far as I could. I wasn't going to be caught by her apricot. But now I wanted to be like Frau Micu, blabbering outrageous things in a soft voice. Didn't she say:

And then I had Emil again, twice . . .

When I brought up the bedding twice that night, I realized that what she had said was getting to me.

If I do decide to go back to the tower block, I'll put on the blouse that waits and sit in the kitchen. Whenever someone gets out of the elevator, the doors clatter like stones one floor up and one below. And on our floor they sound like iron. When I hear iron, I'll go out into the stairwell. Today Albu will come. The first time I was summoned, he showed me his identity card. I got stuck on his photo instead of reading what somebody who squeezes your fingers when he kisses your hand is

213

called by his mother, his wife. There must have been two or three given names, too late, the identity card had been put away. If Albu thinks I ought to disappear, I will tell him the truth:

My grandfather painted the horse outside his house, I've been waiting for you here outside the apartment.

And I'll say the same thing when Paul gets out of the elevator, so that he won't have to start lying right away, until I ask:

Where were you.

As so often before, he'll say:

In my shirt and right with you.

The red Java is glistening with a fresh coat of paint. Quite by accident, just out of boredom, the old man glances at the bush and bends down to Paul's ear. Now Paul stands up and sees me. Why is he buttoning up his shirt.

The trick is not to go mad.